It's Lik

by

Anne O'Gleadra

Beaten Track

www.beatentrackpublishing.com

It's Like This

Published 2014 by Beaten Track Publishing

Copyright © 2014 Anne O'Gleadra

A CIP catalogue record for this book
is available from the British Library.

ISBN: 978 1 909192 79 9

Cover art by Ruth Daniell
Cover design by Jeffrey Ricker and Ruth Daniell
Back cover description by Sarah Brennan-Newell

Beaten Track Publishing,
Burscough, Lancashire.
www.beatentrackpublishing.com

Author's Note:

Please be aware that the following is not about a safe, sane, sober and fully consensual BDSM relationship (although it is not non-consensual). It is instead about two people who want what they want but don't know how to express exactly what that is and the emotional repercussions of their miscommunications.

Please do not use the characters' actions as an outline for healthy BDSM play, as communication is of utmost importance during and around scenes and that is not what goes on here. If you have triggers concerning dubious consent or breath play, I would recommend giving this story a miss. Thank you so much for reading.

For Sarah and Ruth: may there always be cake at midnight.

&

For Nazneen: for bravery.

- Part One -

- 1 -

It's like this: Ian and Brice and Parker and Dylan get off the bus. They've pretended this whole time—just as they've pretended for the last three years—not to notice that Rylan has his arm draped casually over the blue plastic bar at the back of my seat. They pretend not to know that the second we get off the bus (scratch that, he's not even going to wait for that second; it happens before the bus has even come to a complete stop), he'll lower that arm over my shoulders, or drop his hand forward to fuck with my hair and knuckle my neck a little.

He's like that: likes touching me in public, holding hands, kissing, and he does it in that easy way of his—with a Rylan-specific brand of confidence that almost makes people around us forget to look twice. Like he knows, as far as I can tell, what the fuck is going on. That is the difference between us. He knows. I don't.

"So, guess who I saw?" Rylan says, after the bus doors fold shut.

"When?" I ask.

"The point isn't when, douchius, it's who!"

"Seriously? Douchius? Did you just make that up?"

"Once again, not my point. And yes. What do you think?"

"Douche, and all its variants, still reminds me of showering. Grade five French. Stuck in my head."

"Should've washed it out with German, I told you."

"Schnell, schnell."

"Um. OK."

"That's the only German I know. Might have learned it in grade five, too, with all that depressing concentration camp fiction they made us read. So, who did you see?"

* * *

This is how it works. He touches me, like right now, his hand lazy-smug as it does stuff to my neck and hair and shoulder that probably makes a few of our fellow public transit patrons uncomfortable, and we carry on a conversation like the physical aspect of things is not happening. For us, this is normal. It's normal for other couples, too, I assume. Except we're not a couple—at least so far as I can discern. My reasoning is this: to the best of my knowledge, if you're a part of a couple (which, to be fair, I've never actually been), it means that at one point the issue of your relationship status has been declared or at the very least discussed. Like, at one point in time, Partner X says to Partner Y, "So, wanna go out?" or, perhaps if Partner X is slightly more subtle, Partner Y just might suddenly be introduced to others as Partner X's significant other. Or maybe Partner X and Y would discuss the nature of their relationship, what they want from the other, what their joint goals and aspirations are, if they see each other in their futures. Lofty shit like that.

I mean, I could be totally wrong. I could just be an impressionable idiot who's watched too much TV and now incorrectly assumes that that is what relationships are like. Maybe all I'd like is for Rylan to just once infer that we're exclusive. Or that he, I don't know, cares about me when we fuck. Or maybe not when we're fucking because that would be sentimental and weird, but maybe cares about me *because* we fuck. Or we fuck because he cares about me? Anything, really, I just like the thought of those two things going together and I

4

So that's not exactly concrete evidence. The affection though, it is all physical, never verbal, which leads me to think, in my more cranky moments, that we're just fuck buddies. Which makes me worry (OK, obsess) about the fact that I've emotionally invested the last three years in someone who doesn't really want *me*. Oops.

I mean, we're friends, so I know he *likes* me, and the sex...well, the sex is beyond the best thing probably ever, but maybe that's all. Maybe he's just hanging out, waiting for someone who makes him fall in love to come around. Or maybe love doesn't do it for him. What this is? Too many fucking maybes.

* * *

"Pay attention." He's got his bottom teeth just under the ridge of my upper ear. On him, that part of his ear is pierced, a loop that looks like a little silver balancing rainbow sitting on top of his ear. I've never been interested in getting a piercing, although I know he kind of wants me to. But I figure he's got enough for both of us. Three: ear, nipple, tongue. But I'm not into it. It wouldn't suit me, anyway. I'm not that kind of guy. I'm the kind of guy that should be getting a fake tan and giving piggybacks to girls in bikinis. At least that's what Rylan says. None of those items even slightly appeal to me. But Rylan sometimes calls me JCrew to piss me off. Says I belong on a cheesy advertisement. I think (OK, hope) that he means it as a compliment—that at the very least he thinks I'm good looking. So that's nice. I guess.

I don't really get that worked up about it, but objectively I think I'm basically boring looking. I mean, I've got a body and a head and the typical appendages, but I don't have The Look to carry off anything but your average looks-good-in-fitted-sweaters theme, so I leave the making a statement thing to Rylan. And he seems to think he has multiple statements to make, mostly with thrift-store T-shirts, or obnoxious plaid button-ups, or ratty-patch covered blazers and one time a snakeskin cowboy hat that he wouldn't take off for like two weeks.

"Pay attention!" he growls again, closing his teeth over the rim of my ear, hard.

"Dammit, Rylan!" I blush. I should be used to this. So used to this. He likes attention and gets bored easily, meaning he'll usually rely on my presence to get the attention he wants, while simultaneously gaining the attention of half the other passengers as well. "What do you want?"

"I was just asking," he says slowly, flicking his tongue against the cartilage of my ear, which he *knows* gets me every time, "if your boar of a roommate is going to be around this afternoon?"

I know what that means. It means that I am most definitely going to get laid tonight.

"He is not," I respond.

"Excellent," Ry hiss-murmurs into my ear. He squeezes my thigh, and then reaches seductively across me to pull the cord for the next stop. Though why he feels the need to seduce me is beyond me; I was a goner a long time ago.

* * *

We're barely in the door before Rylan is at my neck. He's impatient, I can tell. Not that I mind. Even though he's a little smaller than me, well, not shorter, we're the same height, but definitely slighter, he always takes control. I like that. I've always liked that. I have two younger sisters, and always got good grades and shit, so I boil it all down to a little need for

7

loss of power and try to leave it at that, because I'm pretty sure over-analyzing stuff never got anyone anywhere they wanted to go. Rylan makes a dark, needy sound as he grinds his crotch against my thigh. His teeth are biting harshly into my skin now: he's always been one for instant gratification, for as long as I've known him. He's got my hands pinned above my head, while he rips my sweater upwards off my body, allowing his angry mouth access to more susceptible skin. I am going to be beyond bruised tomorrow.

Shona doesn't get it. She says she's all for a little bit of rough sex, but not like this. She doesn't get how hard it makes me to be slammed against the door, to have Rylan bind my hands within my sweater, then grab me by my belt loops and pull me across the little living room and into my bedroom, half stumbling along the way.

And I only get harder as Rylan strips. We got over the modesty thing a long, long time ago. And now he's just nude and lean and powerful—hungry. My belt replaces my sweater, cuffing my hands together. He hooks the belt over one short wooden bed post, so my arms are twisted, awkward and painful behind me, jutting straight back and up from my shoulder blades, forcing me to kneel, the bed too high to get to. It's obvious we're not going to make it there anytime soon.

Rylan roughly yanks off my pants, releasing my aching cock. He goes down on me immediately and fuck, do I love that tongue stud. But I know he won't let me come yet. He wants to bring me to the brink, and we know each other too well for him to not know when I'm there. So I'm keening upwards into his mouth, his throat, fully aware that just when I'm about to orgasm he'll pull off.

Teeth: just a touch, momentary, and awful but glorious at the same time. I almost break our code. Almost say something, like, "Oh God!" before catching my lip between my teeth and biting down, hard, because we don't talk. He doesn't talk, and I don't talk. We converse as friends, and then we fuck like something more, but we don't mix the two. Not ever. He grins as he slides his mouth off my dick with one last flick of the metal stud. I look at my cock, straining and angry and helpless, and I think that the sight alone might just make me even a little more desperate to come. I love this. Pseudo-powerlessness. Self-imposed imprisonment.

He kisses me then; he loves slavering my own pre-cum across my tongue with his, and I love his body sliding up against mine, even as he plants his hands on my hips to keep me from thrusting, from seeking friction enough to satisfy. His body shifts upwards, and he trails a wet line from his leaking dick up my chest, until it rests at my lips. This will be a new experience: having my hands trapped upwards and incapable of touching him as I swallow his cock, but I really should have foreseen this; our sex has grown increasingly kinky—over this last year especially. I open my mouth obediently and he smiles as he hooks a fist in my hair.

For the first time since we started all this, I feel a twinge of actual fear. The awkward position I'm in would make it next to impossible for me to stand, not without him unhooking my hands from the bedpost for me. As a result, Ry could technically choke me with his cock. My heart rate tells me this freaks me out, but my erection tells me this turns me on, and either way the thought comes too late for me to do anything about it, because he's sliding past my lips and over my tongue and I'm taking it gracefully. I press my tongue to the bottom of his dick to try and relax myself with the familiarity of his feel, his taste. He releases his grip on my hair slightly, and I allow him access to my throat. But he doesn't ease off, he's rigorous and controlling and I can't breathe, and even though I've done

9

this a million times, I've always had access to my hands, to put on his hips, to push him away or pull him closer...

I squeeze my eyes tight. He stops moving, cock huge and thick down my throat. My eyes fly open and I stare up at him, terrified. He stares back, an eyebrow quirked curiously. He grips my chin with one hand, and with the other—he slaps me. This is also new, and sort of scary, but it has the desired effect: I feel like a car that's gotten a jump and I catch a deep inhale through my nose and I trust that he knows what he's doing, and would never do anything to hurt me for real and I should maybe just enjoy.

I know my eyes are wet, not from emotion, but just from the not being able to breathe thing, and my face is probably all red and there's spit and pre-cum around my mouth, possibly on my chin, his and maybe remnants of mine, and as he fucks in and out of my mouth, completely setting his own rhythm. I think of the view I'm creating, and I love it, love the me he brings to the surface, and I would give anything to come right now. But I can't. There's nothing there. And the thought alone isn't *quite* enough. So fucking close, though. And then, as if my thinking about it egged him on, Rylan comes, hard and deep, holding my head over his cock until he's finished and I'm choking awkwardly on semen. Ry pulls out, slowly, lingeringly, until just the head is resting righteously on my tongue. Rylan smirks and I blush and thrust with humiliation and need. He runs the tip of his cock lightly over my lips, like some obscene chap stick, and then suddenly walks out of the room, leaving me caught and aching.

He returns a few minutes later. I've got a desperate boner; he has a fucking sandwich. Lettuce, tomato and cucumber. He hates condiments and he's a fucking vegetarian. Turns out all I can do is kneel here knowing useless shit like that, while he sits cross-legged on the floor, still naked, to watch me. Fuck him.

Christ. I want to break the code, the silence. I want to plead for him to just get me off already. But the expression on his face as he finishes his sandwich, wipes away the crumbs, and slowly starts to jack himself makes it clear that he has other plans.

After what feels like a fucking eternity in cock years, Ry stands and meanders over. He grabs my wrists, and jerks them painfully upwards. I get it though: he wants me to follow. My shoulder joints grumble and thrill at the release but I ignore them. He doesn't lead me very far, just back to the foot of the bed. He unstraps my hands, and I am pathetically tempted to just grab my dick and get there, but I know I'll just be cheating myself out of whatever he's got planned if I do that. He takes my shoulders in his hands and turns me towards him, so my back is against the bed, and indicates that I should crouch down. He curls my hands around two of the vertical wooden bars spaced evenly along the footboard. He encourages my feet outwards, away from each other and away from the bed, before sliding in between my legs. Ah. I get it now. If we could just use words like normal people, I would've figured out that he wanted me to fuck myself on him a lot sooner.

But maybe it's because we do stuff like we do that he doesn't talk, maybe he can't admit it with words—but sometimes I think that if I just figured out how to ask, there's not much Rylan would have a problem admitting. Maybe it's just me with the problem. A confident finger teases at my asshole. I growl or something, because we are so past teasing. For once he obliges and quickly applies lube and works me open with a couple of fingers, but it's getting to be desperate times up here, so I make another noise in the back of my throat urging the proceedings forward. The next thing I know he's moved again. Away from me. Fuck. He's tying my hands to the posts again and I can't help feeling that it's in punishment for my protests. My shoulders are screaming almost as loudly as my dick. But finally, he's ready, lying underneath me, cock hard, eyes watching me almost lazily. I lower myself down, hunching forward a bit to try to release some of the pressure on my shoulders. It hurts a bit from lack of diligent prep, but by now I just need release so bad that I try to push past that. I thrust myself up and down, trying to get the right angle to hit my—fuck.

Yeah. It won't take long now. Genius. He's not doing any of the work, just watching as I pull myself closer and closer, fucking impaling myself on him with need, the pain of the entry becoming a whacked-out sort of pleasure, and then suddenly he's gripping my cock hard, squeezing and pumping and I don't get why until when I thrust down on him once more, and find he's coming and then I'm coming, shoots of the stuff all over my chest, matching the hot spurts inside me. He pulls out. I collapse against the foot of the bed. He's tracing a finger through the cum on my chest, and I'm almost too dead to the world to notice. But not quite.

CUM SLUT.

He writes, his fingertip rearranging the mess on my skin. How lovely. And then he catches my unimpressed expression and laughs, smudging it all out with his palm.

"Just kidding." He grins and kisses me, his lips warm and comforting and happy as they mesh pleasantly with mine. He pulls away the ties at my hands which allows me to melt on the floor, him resting contentedly on top of me, our power dichotomy somehow reversed as he loses consciousness. And I'm exhausted. But I can't sleep.

Just kidding.

Three years of silent fucking, and the first thing he says in terms of sex between us, ever, is, "Just kidding." Not, "Gee, that was fun," or, "By the way, Niles, I really fucking love you," or even, "Was that good?" or, "What can I do better?" or whatever normal people might say after incredible sex. Just...Just kidding. You're not a cum slut. Um...thanks?

* * *

He leaves after a few minutes of sleep: unsticks himself from me, smiles, fucking tousles my hair, and leaves.

He kisses me in public. He kisses me before we fuck. But afterwards, or after the comedown, there's a whole lot of nothing.

I assume I should be acclimatized to this by now. That I should accept the whole situation as "this is how it goes" but of course I don't. Instead, I turn to my favourite activity: obsessing over it in the shower. If I counted up all the frustrated, mind-churning showers I've taken in the last three years, I think the actual number would make me slice my jugular with a plastic fork.

Except for that I know that I wouldn't. Instead I would just be like, "Oh God, that's literally the worst!" and keep right on going with it. It's like Surgeon General's warnings on smokes. It doesn't matter how many of the facts you know, or the statistics, or the risks, or anything; you still just want your fucking smokes. Of course, I quit smoking. But that was only because Rylan told me to. Guess you could say the stronger addiction won out.

He calls early the next morning, like he always does. Even still, if the call comes more than a few days later, I allow that malignant worry to blossom in my brain: maybe that was the last fuck, maybe he's done with me. You know, the usual plaguing fears of an insecure moron. Feeling this way kind of messes with me, because I'm not all that insecure about stuff; like I know I'm not unattractive, and I could have a significant other, *other* than Rylan, if I wanted one (though thinking about being with someone other than him just seems abstract and foreign and a little more terrifying than I'd like to admit), and that I'm smart and we're adults (OK, so we're nineteen, and considered adults by, like, Statistics Canada or the police, or whatever, but I mostly still see myself as, well, a teenager), and I feel pretty autonomous (even though I am totally not, because my parents are paying for my education and rent and everything, really because they say I shouldn't have a job while I'm at school, because they think school should be my focus and all, and yeah—I know I'm spoiled but I really do try not to act it), and I have a steady family life and on and on. So, logically, I shouldn't have this massive uncertainty in my life. And yet, here I am, obsessing.

"I've got tickets for the symphony tomorrow," is what he tells me when he calls.

"The symphony. Really."

"People in this community care about the Arts," he says, adopting a pretentious telemarketer tone.

"And I realize that that is something my formerly redneck Albertan ass can't possibly comprehend...but still, the symphony?"

"You like music."

"Yeah, but—"

"Excellent. Meet me downtown noon-ish? In front of the Douglas Centre."

"Fine. How much are the tickets?"

"I'll take care of it. See you in a bit?"

"Yeah, alright."

- 2 -

I show up in a suit. It's getting a little warm for a jacket and it turns out a suit just makes me feel like an asshole in front of the homeless people hanging around my bus stop. I give the guy closest to me all my change to attempt to assuage my conscience.

"The reason you're always broke, Nigh," Rylan says, appearing from the entrance of the mall and linking his arm with mine, "is that you choose to throw your money away. They're just going to spend it on drugs and alcohol." His tone is facetious and mock-WASPy. He casually drops a twenty into the basket of a run-down woman with a mangy German shepherd before leading me deftly to the crosswalk.

"Are you wearing a tux underneath that jacket?" he demands. "Because I could swear those are your grad shoes..."

"It's just a suit. I thought it was appropriate, considering this is one of your so-called cultural society events."

"It sure is. Hence why I feel the need to add some clothing of the non-conformist variety."

He's wearing about six layers of different, tight-fitting T-shirts and sweaters, all topped off with a zip-up hoodie, none of which seem to increase his bulk (or lack thereof) even slightly.

"You look plain old hipster to me," I bite back.

"Better than being a sell-out to the previous generation."

"Spoken like the true child of a broken home."

"Says the offspring of the bourgeoisie."

I don't exactly have a comeback for that one.

* * *

The symphony is something by Dvořák that I won't venture a guess at pronouncing. Rylan has been saying it at every opportunity, because before he quit (or, took a break from, as he likes to say) uni, he took a semester of Russian, and feels that this entitles him to adopt a pseudo-Czech inflection. We're part of the one percent of the people in here under the age of, oh, I don't know, dead? Everywhere you look is a sea of white hair and everywhere you turn, you almost knock the walker out from under some retiree. My thoughts on the matter are confirmed when I open the program and find an ad: "Have you put the Symphony Orchestra in *your* will?" Oh, Jesus.

"A bit morbid, eh?" Rylan grins, comfortably dropping his arm on my shoulders. We're seated. The auditorium is a neoclassical throwback, complete with nude Grecian figures over the massive doorways, sporting the masks of comedy and tragedy. There is next to no space between us and the row in front of us. I'm glad we sat early so I don't have to disrupt the string of seniors whom I'm sure will gradually materialize in the empty seats to our sides.

"Hardly!" I rebut, sarcastically. "There's nothing I'd rather think about on an afternoon out than planning for my future demise."

"You're from Calgary. You don't know shit." He grins, affectionately.

Whenever Ry's losing an argument, he pulls the Alberta card, even though I've been here since sixth grade. I didn't meet Rylan 'til tenth grade, though. We went to different elementary schools, and even though I must've seen him in the halls during our first two years at high school, it wasn't until our English 10 teacher, who was still into organized seating

16

(pods and everything), put us together that we actually got to know each other.

Neither of us subscribed to a particular social clique in high school. Of course there were cliques, but none were particularly vicious (other than to the unfortunate few) like in teen movies or anything. I was mostly friends with Brice and Parker and a few other guys I've mostly lost contact with, besides being like, Facebook friends, and he was mostly friends with Ian and Dylan. So when Rylan and I started hanging out, we just sort of threw them all together, and everything worked out pretty well.

What I'm getting at is that stuff with Rylan and me hasn't always been the way it is now. We honestly did just start out as friends. I never saw any of this coming. Not until it was pretty much happening. The first time...well, it wasn't really "the first time," because that sounds like sex and I guess that depends how you define sex, but either way the first incident thing, happened over Christmas break the year we met. There was Brice's parents leaving a day early for their holiday (he was flying out the next day to meet them), alcohol, the group of us guys, and a whole lot of stupidity.

I don't remember what we did, besides from scratching the hell out of the pool table, and spilling cheap vodka mixed with chocolate milk (this was a mistake) all over Brice's parents' new carpet and then, of course, the ritual passing out in various parts of the house (Ian, our resident over-drinker, in the bathroom) around three or four in the morning.

I was in the guest room. I know that for sure. I was sprawled diagonally on the quilt of a single bed, the angle, mixed with my being drunk, obscuring my perception of the room. I woke up when Rylan entered a few hours later. 7:28 was glowing on the digital clock, which made the guest room feel even more like a hotel room than the washed out flowered walls and brass am at least eighty percent sure that that is sort of normal. But honestly, I'd settle for him saying *anything* about our sex life.

Shona says I should just talk to him about it and obviously, cerebrally, I know that. But how does one enquire into this kind of situation, because, "So, Ry, are we like...*together*-together?" doesn't quite cut it. Because if we are, well, together-together, and have been for the three years that I think we have been together, he might get pretty pissed at me being in the dark about the whole thing, whereas, if we're *not* together, and we're just screwing around, then voicing it might make it go away. And no matter how much I may bitch about the whole thing, I most definitely do *not* want it to go away. Or stop. Or change in any way—with the possible exception of me knowing what the fuck is going on.

I know the whole thing is ridiculous. It totally is. And even if I did somehow forget just how ridiculous the whole thing is, Shona draws me a pretty clear diagram of the magnitude of its absurdity every time we hang out.

"How are you and your ambiguous friend?" she likes to ask.

Usually this results in me flopping forlornly on her bed and whining that I wish I knew what I was to him. Most of the time, I have a pretty clear idea. Usually, I can lull myself into very-almost believing that he's mine and I'm his and all that, because he really is super affectionate, and I mean, everyone we know knows we're together. Like, all of our friends, other than Shona, sometimes call Rylan my boyfriend to me, and I assume when they talk to him I'm called his boyfriend? Maybe? Though it's really not enough to settle things, because we were all friends before Rylan and I ever started hooking up, so mainly, our friends just refer to us both by name, Niles and Rylan, the "boyfriend" word only ever surfacing as a sort of joke.

lamps already made it feel. Looking back, it seems like such an ironic, innocent time of day to have one's first homosexual encounter. Or any-sexual encounter, for that matter, seeing as we were the kind of guys that mostly just hung out with guys; we were still pretty awkward and immature around girls.

I remember I checked the time because I didn't know what he was doing there, or I thought it was time to go...somewhere. Mostly I was almost still drunk, or at least tired enough to feel drunk. When Rylan didn't supply me with any information, I dropped my head back down. I was really fucking tired. I heard him inhale, deeply, and I think now that he was trying to steady himself for what he was about to do (he got over that need for self-assurance in about a week, because I haven't heard him take a great, stabilizing breath since), but I didn't know that at the time.

"Are you drunk?" he asked, suddenly right next to the bed, looking down at me.

"No," I half-lied.

"Good," he responded, his voice rough but sure. And then he was over me, thighs gripped tight, straddling mine, his hands anchoring mine to the bland quilt at my sides. He mashed his lips against mine without a second thought.

For what seemed like a full minute, but for what was probably only a second, I didn't get it. I didn't know what he was doing. I remember my brain trying to process what was happening, seeing his eyes clamped closed and scrunched, and feeling his inexperienced mouth connect with mine.

I didn't get that he was kissing me until I did, and then my first reaction was to wonder *why* he was kissing me. Clueless suggestions bombarded my mind: maybe he thinks I'm a girl, or maybe he's sleepwalking, or maybe I'm having some fucked-up Freudian dream that I should never tell anyone about. But finally, I got it. He was kissing *me*. Rylan was persistent. I mean, I wasn't giving him shit in return, but he was kissing my lips over and over again, not knowing if he could use tongue. It was therefore darting awkwardly out before retreating worriedly into his mouth again. I had to make a choice. I could push him off. I knew we could both plead drunkenness and never speak of this again, or else I could kiss him back.

In the end, my dick made my choice for me. Him rubbing against me as he attacked my mouth got me pretty hard, pretty quick. Looking back, I think that that reaction was probably the crotch friction in combination with my hands being held down, but I hadn't really clued into my more...non-resistant side at that point. So: an erection, and the terrifying realization, "Holy shit! I'm a fag!"

Because a guy was kissing me and it was making me hard. In the end, I figured that since I was fucked already, I might as well kiss back. So I did. At that moment, I heard the only sigh of relief that I have ever heard Rylan make. Within minutes, his tongue was officially done with hanging out in his mouth, and so I tried to kiss him back with tongue too, mainly to disguise the fact that I didn't know what I was doing. It was messy, and awkward, and saliva wasn't really staying where you mainly want saliva to stay, but we were undoubtedly kissing.

I don't know if it was his first kiss. It was awkward enough to be, but I couldn't say for sure. I don't ask him about things like kissing, or girlfriends, or relationships or sex, because God forbid we actually address anything. It was definitely mine, though. I remember thinking, "Holy fuck, I'm kissing!" which gradually morphed into, "So, this is what kissing is like," until my cock took over my ability to think and we just kept rubbing up against each other, kissing (mouths only, we didn't think to explore necks or ears or anything) until we came: me then him, but not by much.

After a minute or two, Rylan started a tradition we follow to this day: he got up, wiped his mouth with the back of his hand, smiled, and left, leaving me with a red face and sore lips and sticky boxers and a ridiculous amount of questions, not the least of which was, "What the fuck is going on?" I was sixteen. Our friends were straight. Fuck, I had assumed *we* were straight. And hours later, over Cinnamon Eggos and video games, we both acted like nothing had happened, like we both weren't commando under our jeans. And so I never brought it up. And he never brought it up. And when things escalated with every chance that we got, I felt more and more unable to actually talk about it.

Which leaves me here: intermission at a symphony, having ignored the entire first half, like I ignore everything in life, because I refuse to address this one little...who am I kidding, the *only* fucking issue I have. But I don't have time to think about that now, because Rylan's leading me with determination to an unmarked door, and I'm pretty sure he's hoping we can jack each other off before the lights in the foyer begin to flash.

* * *

"You know, you can bring your ambiguous friend along, if you like."

"Hmm?"

I'm at Shona's pre-gaming. She's got her hair with that hill thing at the front, which really just reminds me of a Corythosaurus more than anything. I don't get it. But Shona likes it and she's subtly creative with make-up, and while her shirt is cleavage-y, it's not tacky cleavage-y. She looks nice.

"Rylan," she clarifies. "I don't mind if you invite him. I mean, no offense or anything, but I'm kind of looking to get laid tonight anyway...so I don't mind if you want him to come. It will make me feel less guilty if I ditch you."

"Shona, you are a slut and I love you."

"No way, Nigh," she protests. "Sluts go to the club looking for meaningless sex weekly. I go to the club looking for meaningless sex after a devastating break-up with my boyfriend of, if you'll recall, a year and three-quarters."

His name was Jesse. He was...alright? Kinda bland, but Shona made it clear she didn't put a lot of stock in what I considered "alright" relationship-wise.

"Riiiight. Because you never had meaningless sex while you and Jesse were together, or anything..."

"Not, like, on the regular! Now, silver, gold, or black with little stars?" She's holding up hoop earrings.

"Fuck if I know."

"Anyone ever mention you are the most useless gay BFF ever?"

"You. Daily."

Shona grins and kisses—more like smooches—my cheek.

"Oh right! Glad someone's keeping you in check."

- 3 -

I end up calling Ry. He sounds pleasantly surprised, seeing as I usually leave him in charge of making the plans. Which I guess is a lot to put on him, considering we see each other pretty much every day.

Before I met him, I didn't get that. I thought girls who spent every day with their boyfriends were needy and didn't have a life of their own or something. But I get it now. What it comes down to is this: he's my best friend and my favourite person to hang out with, so, if possible, why wouldn't we hang out? He says he thinks Ian and Parker are working, but he'll call the other guys and see if they're up for it. I'm glad that he and I never really, like, lost our friends—that we didn't get sucked into the relationship vortex. Looking back, I'm surprised we didn't. We kind of kept the whole "him and me" thing under wraps for about six months or so, and we were never technically out when we were in high school (that just introduces way more issues than we were interested in dealing with—another one of those things we seemed to decide on without ever talking about), but after a while, Rylan began to slip up on purpose. When we were hanging out with just Ian, Brice, Parker and Dylan (who Rylan takes great delight in referring to collectively as DRIP), it was a bit different. Ry was subtle at first. He would push me over if I beat him at Mortal Kombat, or MarioKart or whatever, or he'd sit closer to me than maybe was necessary when we were all hanging out. It weirdly kind of excited me, like a crush coming to fruition, I guess. It felt like proof. That even if we weren't talking about it, it wasn't a secret, either. I felt, or, maybe I pretended to myself that he was, I don't know, staking a claim or something—and that I most definitely liked.

The guys ignored it. They ignored it when Ry would card a hand through my hair, or over my back, or, you know, cuddle up to me while we all watched a movie. I figure they all had, "Are you guys like gay or something?" lodged in their throats, but none of them were willing to ask first. They just waited for someone else to say something. So, when no one did, and when Rylan and I refused to offer any information, I guess they just kind of grew into it. They're all so chill about it now, no one would guess that there was ever any awkwardness about it at all. I mean, obviously there was, the first few months, like...uncomfortable shifting and sidelong looks, and Brice has a horrible problem with blushing, but, I don't know. I probably don't even appreciate how good I've got it.

It's the same with my family. I never really came out to them either. I just started spending more and more time alone with Rylan and...they just sort of figured it out. I remember the first day my mom referred to Rylan as my boyfriend I was so startled that I think I knocked my cup of limeade all over the kitchen island. I mean, I guess I just had always assumed that I had kept them kind of separate, like, I figured if I didn't act like a stereotype then they wouldn't catch on, and I kinda bristled whenever Ry tried to touch me in front of them and stuff. I obviously didn't give them enough credit—that, and just because you keep things separate in your head doesn't mean they are actually separate in real life. And my mom is just kind of awesome: instead of trying to sit me down and have a big talk about it, she just stuck it out there to let me know that she was cool with it and I had nothing to worry about. I don't know if they had a more direct talk with my younger sisters or not, but Matilda never made a thing about it, and Kya's too young to know whether or not a thing is normal.

So, my family = rad, but Rylan's family...they're fucked. You know how there's families that are dysfunctional, and yet adorable in their dysfunctionality? Like quirky dysfunctional? Rylan's family is not like that. They are just fucked. His folks split (divorced? maybe? I'm not really clear as to whether or not they were ever married? Not that that matters, but I honestly just don't know) when he was a kid. His dad's kind of a loser and his mom's a total alcoholic. He moved back and forth between them a lot growing up, but mostly ended up with his mom. She did the whole, like, spending his swimming registration fees on booze and stuff, or ending up puking in the bathroom when he tried to have us all sleep over— embarrassing, awkward, private stuff like that. He's pretty pissed at her for a lot of things, so he moved out as soon as he'd saved some money and he doesn't see her. Ry says she can deal with her fuck ups herself. I don't know if I necessarily agree with him on that, but...it's not my area to touch. If he thinks he needs her out of his life in order for him to live like he wants, then I don't really think I can get in the way of that.

I've only ever met Rylan's mom a couple of times. She seemed friendly but she might have just been wasted. I was only fourteen or fifteen and I didn't have a lot of experience around drunk people, and she's one of those people who drinks so constantly that it's hard to tell when she's drunk. Ry says it is easier just to assume she is. He calls her a functioning alcoholic. She has a job, she goes to work, goes home, drinks until she passes out, gets up and does it all over again. Rylan sees his dad, the EI king, once in a while, though. They like to bowl together, but that's about all his dad does. I doubt Ry's folks know that he's gay. (Or bi. Or whatever. Because we've never actually had that conversation. Jesus Christ, what is wrong with me?)

My family adores him. My little sisters attack him every time he walks through the door, even Matilda (who we call Attila (the Hun), which arose a long time ago from TV, I think? I can't actually remember? and it just stuck) who is sixteen, and would probably be considered too tall to be jumping on people. Whatever though, Ry likes the attention. If we ever break up (if we can break up, seeing as we're not officially together), I think it will devastate them as much as it will me. Kya, my youngest (and yes, definitely accidental) sister, who's seven, tells people she's got two older brothers. This tends to confuse things later, if they see Rylan and me acting more than brotherly towards each other.

* * *

Brice meets us at the club. Sandi, his current girlfriend (read: brunette airhead who won't last two months) follows him in, dressed about as skankily as one can dress—just the way Brice likes them. I think he's one of those guys who, when he turns about thirty-four, will suddenly grow up and marry a wholesome pharmacist and have a couple of kids and a big house in the Uplands and have a cabin on the lake, but…well, right now he's into being, in general, an asshole, and drinking too much and driving too fast and, most of all, having not strictly safe sex with a variety of women. He gropes Sandi's ass while we wait for the dance floor to fill up.

Rylan buys Shona and I pornstars because they are on special. He has his usual rum and Coke, and Brice downs three Jägerbombs in quick succession. I'm not that interested in getting drunk tonight, but everyone else seems to be. Shona's eyes are skimming the club for, well, anyone to bang, pretty much. She and I are sitting on tall stools attached to the floor, and Rylan is standing behind me, pressed right up against me. He's such a sucker for physical contact. Not that I'm exactly complaining. A group of about ten women comes in, wearing pretty much nothing but lingerie—like corsets and fishnets, and I don't get it for a moment until I notice that one near the back, looking pretty fucking embarrassed, is wearing a veil and a tiara and a big pink, plastic necklace that says "BRIDE."

The girls approach the bar and, with the exception of the bride-to-be, are being pretty damn raucous. Brice whistles at them, and Sandi looks confused and hurt. I feel bad for her. She probably thinks Brice's asshole act is, well, an act. It's not. Not even close. When it comes to girls, Brice is pretty much a douchebag. We all move down to the dance floor. It's finally started to fill up a bit, and we're not interested in listening to the girls beg free drinks in honour of the occasion. Brice and Sandi immediately find a quasi-secluded corner in which they grind up against each other and make out. Shona and Rylan and I just dance. Clubbing is such a strange phenomenon: music so loud it hurts, everyone pretty much just looking around for someone to fuck. I don't need someone to fuck, seeing as I already have someone, so it's not an activity I particularly enjoy. I get bored of dancing fast. I'm basically just wingmanning for Shona until she finds *herself* someone, and then I intend on indicating to Rylan that we could be elsewhere, like, for instance, in a bed, or against a wall, or over a countertop.

A short but kind of hot dude dances his way up to Shona. She grins at him and doesn't hesitate to make him feel welcome. I start to calculate the number of songs it will take before I can shout "you good?" into her ear and take off with Rylan in tow, when a couple of girls start moving in on Rylan and me. He's good-natured and grins and wiggles his hips and does stupid-adorable fake dance moves with the one that seems interested in him. Not knowing what else to do, I kind of half-heartedly dance with her friend. I wonder if we're both wingmanning tonight.

I'm considering asking her when Rylan unexpectedly grabs the back of my head and pulls me in, harshly, so his lips are against mine and his tongue is plunging into my mouth and the girls are standing looking at us kind of bewilderedly before smiling and giving us thumbs up and walking away. Rylan pulls back and grins at me—he thinks he's pretty fucking funny—and then he tugs harshly at my nipple through my shirt for no good reason and says something about getting more drinks, and struts away, leaving me vaguely horny and alone. Well, alone for about three seconds, that is, because the next thing I know Shona is pulling herself really close to me, rubbing her body against mine, and I get that the guy who made a move on her has been deemed creepy. I put my hands on her waist and pull her in close until the guy gets the message and begins his search elsewhere. Shona mouths "thank you" and rolls her pretty, made-up eyes.

I look around for Rylan. When I spot him, I'm a little surprised to see the bride from the bachelorette party whispering in his ear. He beams and offers her his arm like some nineteenth century throwback. She links hers with his, holding onto his bicep and they walk down the steps together. Rylan seeks us out, passes Shona and me our drinks and then turns back to the bride, one arm circling her waist and the other clasping one of her hands. They dance like they're at a fucking wedding and not a club, at all. His cheek lights against hers and he shout-whispers something into her ear and she tips her head back, laughing, her long throat exposed. I feel sick and stupid, because, despite her tacky attire and her gaggle of loud friends whooping behind her, they look really...beautiful together and I'm swamped with this guilt, like, what if I'm keeping Rylan from something he wants or should have or would have if it wasn't for me? What if I'm an obligation for bringing him home to my family, or just a handy thing to have around until he finds someone like this girl? And it's not like I'm actually worried something's going to happen, like, she's getting married and this is just a bachelorette party and it's just a club and it's just been going on for a few songs and I'm supposed to be hanging out with Shona, anyway, but I can't help the tight, bitter nerves that coil in my guts.

Shona's watching them, I mean, we don't stop dancing, but she's watching them and then watching me. I try to smile at her like I'm having fun and she looks like she feels kinda bad for me, but she's also still looking around, hoping to make eye contact with someone who she can take home. I'm kind of pissed about it, even though Shona is nothing if not upfront about what she wants, and it's not like I didn't know what tonight was about. Finally, after another couple of songs, Rylan starts to make his way back over to me. I'm embarrassingly relieved. He grins at me, and then I notice the bride's behind him, and he's holding their hands to the small of his back so they don't get separated as they *keep fucking walking* over to the bar where he buys her a fucking drink, and then some new guy encroaches on Shona, and she gives me the thumbs up saying that she's happy with him, and I'm good to go, but Jesus *fuck*, I don't have anyone to go home *with*, seeing as I've been ditched for someone who's about to get fucking married, areyouabsolutelyfucking*kidding*me!

I watch Rylan and his fucking wife down two shots of tequila, drop their limes into their shot glasses, and make their way back to the dance floor, where Rylan fucking spins her and dips her and they laugh. I walk right up behind her. He's got his hand dangerously close to her ass, and it takes him a couple of seconds before he sees me, but when he does, he just smiles. I glare at him impatiently and he looks sort of confused. I seriously want to get out of here, doesn't he get that? And I feel like I should be entitled to going home with my boyfriend, but instead I just feel like I'm having a fucking temper tantrum or something, because I just fucking stalk out of there and leave. And I'm acting irrationally, which makes me feel embarrassed and ashamed and humiliated, and that just makes me more frustrated, so I just fucking get into one of the waiting taxis and give the cabby my address. As the driver pulls a U-turn in front of the club, I can't help but look for Rylan, like maybe he's wondering where I got to. But I don't see him because he's a selfish bastard and I'm a pathetic idiot.

- 4 -

It's barely past midnight by the time I get home and I'm too fucking mad to do anything. The worst part is that I don't know if I'm even justified in being mad. Like, it's not like we've ever established that we're not allowed to do whatever the fuck we want with other people. Who knows, maybe he goes to the club and hooks up with randoms all the time? I throw myself dramatically onto my bed, wishing I could phone Shona but I can't even do that because she's probably making out with the guy on the dance floor by this point and I feel like such a useless idiot. Why haven't I just asked him?

Seriously. All I needed to do to avoid this was ask him what was between us, let him put me out of my misery. But I didn't. Because what if he'd said...What if he said that—Jesus. That he was just in it for the sex. He can't just be in it for the sex. It would end me if he said that. Because. I fucking love him. I don't ever *ever* admit it, but I do. And I'd forgive him anything if he'd just fucking show up and...I don't know. Everything's so fucked up. Usually, I am composed, honest to God, I have control over myself. I can watch my drinking, and what I eat, and I make sure that I get off my ass on a semi-regular basis. But when it comes to him, I'm an absolute idiot, and I don't think, and I just give in even if I promise I won't. Which I've given up promising because I know I'll just give in anyway. Fuck.

I don't know how, but I somehow fall asleep. I only know I was asleep and not still tormenting myself because now I am definitely awake and Rylan is standing in my doorway. He smells drunk. He walks towards my bed, not really staggering, but not close to sober, either. And he pulls off his shirt and he unbuckles his pants and lets them fall and he scoops off my blanket and I'm just lying there, in my boxers. And he licks his lips and straddles me and brings his face in close to mine and even though I feel like I hate him I let him because I'm just so fucking thankful he's here.

He leaves dark, bruising hickeys all over my chest before stripping me of my boxers and bending up my knees and quickly preparing me and then going for it. It hurts a bit and I grit my teeth, but that fades in a second and he's leaning over me, kissing me hard, and fucking me harder. He jacks me quickly, and of course I get hard. And he looks at me like he's thinking something that he considers saying, but he doesn't. He just tightens his fingers around my dick, which hurts but it's me, so I like it, and we're both getting closer, everything's speeding up, and then the next thing I know, he's got his free hand up at my face, forcing my nostrils closed and I'm gasping for air in surprise, but he keeps his mouth tight over mine.

It hits me that he's suffocating me. My lungs and my throat burn and I panic, but he keeps on fucking me—deep, rapid jabs, and jacking me and my body somehow keeps on responding, and I swear it's even more sensitive than it usually is because all I can pay attention to is that I need air and I need to come, and it's like these are the only two needs I'll ever have and one's approaching, but if I don't get the other soon, I'll die. Literally, I'll die. And he grips me impossibly harder and I need to breathe, and I toss my head violently in an effort to get away, but he keeps kissing me, blocking out my chance for air with his tongue, and then he's coming and I'm coming, more than coming, I'm igniting, pouring out harder than I ever knew I could, like it's the last thing I'm ever going to do. And then he's breathing into my mouth and I'm drinking in the oxygen, which isn't enough, but will have to be enough, and he pulls out, leaving me sweaty and vacant with lungs aching until finally, sweetly, he moves his mouth away and I draw my own breath, and the air blisters the whole way down.

We're collapsed. Even if he's smaller than me, I feel like he's crushing me, I'm so weak. He presses kisses to my sweaty forehead, nuzzles my cheek, and suckles at my ear until I'm not awake anymore.

* * *

He's still here. When I wake up next morning, Rylan's still lying on top of me, head curled awkwardly into my shoulder and neck. I shift slightly and that wakes him and he looks down at me. A few hours must have passed because he doesn't seem drunk anymore. He smiles contentedly at me, and rolls off me, propping himself up on one elbow. He keeps his other hand on my stomach. It drifts casually over my ribs and up to my chest.

I do believe this is the closest we've ever come to pillow talk. He licks his lips. Swallows. Doesn't speak.

Am I supposed to say something? Is that what he's waiting for? Because I can't find a single word.

His palm finds my jaw, curls around it. He moves in closer to me, our bodies touching, and he kisses the corner of my mouth. I find myself reacting mechanically, but I'm too late and I end up kissing air and not him. Not that I know if I want to kiss him. He tilts his forehead into my temple.

Breathing on me. Breathing...that's kind of cruel, isn't it?

I don't like the way he is looking at me. I can't define it and I close my eyes, but I know I don't like it. His lips glance off my ear. I don't move. His hand relocates to my hip, gentle and placating all the way down, but it doesn't work. I'm shaky and disoriented.

He's waiting. I know it somehow, even if I don't know what he wants, and even if I did I couldn't give it to him. I couldn't give a single fucking thing at this moment. He has me all, anyway. Whether I want it or not.

He whispers something into my ear, it might be my name, but I don't catch it. His hand won't stop moving over me, slow and fucking tender, like nothing I'm used to at all. Maybe he feels badly, maybe he wants to do it again and is trying to coax me or maybe I won't ever be able to figure him out so I should just give this up. My lip is between his lips. He drags his mouth across the line of my cheek bone and then his tongue traces the bone behind my ear. He kisses the spot in front of my ear. But he doesn't use his teeth even once. This isn't us. We don't behave this way. Maybe I wanted it before but not anymore.

Or maybe that's all bullshit. We both know that if he went for my cock right now I'd let him fuck me. That's what I do, or that's what we do. *That's* us.

He uses his arm to pull me close against him, tight and there's so much...contact. He kisses my face five or six times, and I don't respond and he sighs or groans but it's not quite voiced. He peels himself off me.

I watch him as he puts on his clothes, so normally. He's at the door. He turns, looks at me watching him. He walks out. All I can do is turn away, unable to process anything except that he's gone and I'm aching.

And then suddenly he's back and he's kissing my mouth, sideways and awkwardly and he's saying he'll call me in a bit, OK? And I'm nodding, dumbly, and closing my eyes and he's running fingertips over my forehead and in a few minutes I know I'll be alone again.

"Remember how I told you I'd tell you when it was time to draw the line?" Shona says. I can picture her: she's probably half-dressed, pajama pants and bra, cereal bowl on lap, cross-legged. Phone caught between her chin and shoulder causing neck pain she'll whine at me to knead out later.

"Yes. And I remember telling you how I would ignore you telling me to draw the line."

"Babe." Shona never uses her serious voice, but she is using it now. "You need to draw the line."

I don't respond.

"Niles, come on. This isn't me being an asshole. I know I'm not super Team Rylan but I swear I'm trying to be objective and—he...he fucking tried to strangle you."

"It wasn't like that," I protest.

"Wow, because that doesn't sound exactly like every abuse-victim-in-denial ever." And I know it's serious because Shona doesn't do caring, but here she is.

"Well, it wasn't. He didn't try to strangle me."

"Suffocate, then. Any way you look at it, it's fucking weird."

"I didn't tell him to stop," I mumble, stupidly.

"Oh, and when would you have gotten that in? Before or after he was choking you with his tongue?"

"Shona, please."

"Look. Or, like, listen, OK? This has breached the kinky line. This is the here-there-be-monsters jagged edge of the map. This is the point of no return. Luckily, you've got me holding onto the back of your shorts, pulling you back onto dry land. Niles, please. This. Cannot. Go on."

I sigh. "I know."

There's a long pause as she chews a mouthful of cereal. "You're not going to stop, are you?"

I swallow. "No."

"I can't fucking believe this."

I don't answer.

"What do I have to do, Niles? I'm seriously freaked out, OK? He was drunk. He fucking *cut off your air supply*, and—"

"And I didn't make a single move to stop it. He didn't even have my arms tied down. I'm stronger than him. I could've pushed him off if I'd wanted to."

"That's bullshit. He's got such a creepy power over you! I hate it! Why don't you get that you could've been *killed*!"

"He wouldn't hurt me."

"He already has. Just because I don't comment on it doesn't mean I haven't seen the evidence." The sentences start coming faster now, and I know we're either going to fight it out or let it drop, but I don't know which yet.

"I like it."

"You lik*ed* it." Shona's voice is tight, loud, final. "Now, it's fucked."

"I love him."

A pause. She sighs. Finally, "I know."

"How?" I never told her.

"I'm not an idiot. It's messed up. Look, just...will you get him to wear a fucking condom or something? If he's not going to kill you while fucking you, I don't want him to give you something that will kill you later on."

"What's the point? I've got whatever he's got."

"But you don't have whatever he might *get*."

I don't want to hear it. I don't want to think about the possibility of him kissing-fucking-teasing-tying *any*one else, *ever*. I'm sick. I'm fucking sick. Hell. I wish Shona wasn't right.

"Fine."

"OK." We breathe at each other for a minute or so. "Look, babe," she says, finally, "I've gotta go. Call me? You know?"

36

"I know."

"Love you."

"You too."

"More than he fucking does." She hangs up.

I feel like puking.

* * *

He calls later, as promised.

"Helloooooo, Captain Niles." He calls me that sometimes. Don't know why. It seems to me his cheeriness should be forced but it comes across as completely natural.

"Hey," is all I can muster.

"Soooo, are you coming over?"

I don't know I don't know I don't know.

"Yeah, alright."

"OoooK. Pick up a vocabulary on the way over, yeah?" he teases.

I hang up.

* * *

My hands shake as I pay for the condoms. I feel like such an idiot. I've been having sex for over three years, and I have never used a condom, never even thought about it. Well, except for when Shona presses for it, but in the past I've always found ignoring her works quite well. I probably look like a quivering virgin. I can't look the bored salesgirl in the eye; I'm such a douchebag.

As soon as I'm out of the store, I rip open the pack and shove a couple condoms in my back pocket. I don't know what to do with the rest of them so I throw them into a trash can. What the hell is wrong with me?

For some reason when I get to Rylan's I want to buzz up, even though I have his spare set of keys. I don't buzz up, of course, don't even know the code, and I don't want him thinking something's up anyway. There's nothing up. I'm just utterly fucked up, that's all.

He smiles toothily at me from the couch when I open the door to his place, and he looks genuinely happy to see me. He always does. It's probably why I keep coming back.

He's got Scrabble out on the coffee table, all set up. Bring a vocabulary, ha-ha, he thinks he's funny at any rate. He holds out the Crown Royal bag he keeps the letters in, and I dutifully pull out seven tiles.

"You can go first," he informs me, only after inspecting his letters, making sure he's not giving me too much of an advantage.

I play "ORDAIN." Scrabble sucks when you don't have any letters worth more than two points and the board is the absolute last thing on your mind.

He plays "SALIVA" and wiggles his eyebrows at me.

I know where this is going. I play "VOUCH."

He screws his mouth up at his letters for a while, dropping them into different places on the little wooden stand. Finally, his face lights up and he silently pieces his word together from the end up. He plays "HANDLE."

And then suddenly he's crawling over the table and on top of me. So basically the shortest game of Scrabble actually ever.

He's got me pressed into the carpet, mouth hot over mine and I want him. Every damn time I want him, because every time is a reaffirmation that I *mean* something. He shoves his hands under my shirt, grates them over my ribs.

We're panting like we've never done this before, like our bodies are new to each other, anticipation coating the air and I know how I'm so hungry for him all the time, but I don't understand how he's so hungry for me. He grinds against my already desperate dick, and goes straight for my belt, impatient as ever.

For a second I freeze. He doesn't seem to mind. Somehow my fingers know what to do: they scramble around behind me and shakily dip into the pocket. I clench a condom in my fist, which probably renders it ineffective, but I can't help myself.

He notices, or notices the movement at least. He grabs my fists and plants them firmly above my head, streaking his teeth across my neck. I arch up into him, allowing him all the access he wants.

He uncurls my fists, discovers the condom, and stares for...a full forever. Or thirty seconds or something.

I don't move. He doesn't move. He just holds it.

I don't breathe.

And then suddenly he climbs off of me completely. Stands. Drops the condom on the floor beside me.

"You need to go," is all he says.

- 5 -

I think I'm numb. My pulse is jackhammering and my hands are clammy and my stomach is contorting and I almost fall down the stairs in my hurry to escape.

Fuck. Fuck. Fuckity fuck, *fuck*. I am such a douchy-clueless-idiot-mess. Do I seriously have to fuck everything up *every* time? It would have been so worth it to just forget the condom, to let him fuck me because it's too late, anyhow. Anything he has I have and anything he has I want because I just want *him*. Jesus, I'm seriously deranged and FUCK. I almost run into someone. I'm not running though, I feel like I am, but I'm not. My feet seem sensible, hard against the pavement, fast, but grounded and my body just follows along, head down, not caring if I slam into anything. I can't do this. I want to turn around and run up the stairs and fucking beg or something. But I don't. I rebuckle my belt, tighter, pretend it's him, teasing me in. God, I want him. Concentrate. Concentrate. Concentrate. On what, I have no fucking idea. I need to get out of here. Off this road, out of this neighbourhood, and I can't go home, I can't be around. Cody will be there and he's such a loud, present, stupid ape of a roommate, and I can't deal.

I wait at a bus stop. I scrounge around in my pocket for change because I think my bus pass fell out somewhere. At his place. On his floor. Probably just after he kissed me for the last fucking time ever. Though I don't think he even did kiss me, it was just the thing with my neck. I cover it with my hand. I

41

want to look down my shirt, find the hickeys, I can't ever let them fade. Shit, I'm so messed up. Who thinks like this?

Across the street I see the 16 bus. I know that bus because I used to take it home, every day. Home as in my family's house. I run across the street, even though the walk light is definitely not on, and I dump my change in the slot and I collapse on a seat. I bang my head against the window, and I don't think. I don't even allow myself to think a single fucking thing, because it will just prove how crazy I am.

* * *

No one's home. Of course they're not. It's only like one o'clock. My parents are both at work and my sisters are still at school. I mean, I have a key, so it's not like I can't get in, but once I'm in, I'm alone again. Fuck. I think of calling Shona, but I don't want to hear anything so…true as what she will feed me at the moment. I want to just pretend the whole thing was one of those fucked-up dreams I have sometimes. I sit on the couch and turn on the TV and look out the front window. I channel surf without absorbing a single thing until I hear the Volvo in the driveway.

My mom rushes into the kitchen and drops her purse on the counter and briefcase on the floor. She starts when she sees me standing awkwardly in the doorway between the kitchen and family room.

"Niles!" She puts a hand to her chest. "Sweetheart, you scared the hell out of me."

"Sorry."

She flutters over and her hands land on my shoulders, which she squeezes before kissing my cheek. "Haven't seen you in a while. Everything OK?"

"Yep," I find myself lying. "Just missed you."

She laughs and gently swats at my cheek. "Ha-funny-ha. Do you need money or something? We gave you some for the month, didn't we?" She looks momentarily upset. "I was sure we did!"

"No, Mom, you did!" I assure her. "I seriously just came to see you guys."

"Oh." She runs a hand over her hair. "Well. I'm glad you did. And I wish I could stay and chat, but I promised Tillie I'd pick her up from school. I was just popping home to grab an apple—board meeting ran late and I am absolutely starving."

"She hates it when you call her that," I say, shaking my head.

Mom snorts. "I birthed her. I'll call her whatever I want."

"Why don't I go get her?"

Mom smiles, looking pleased and relieved. "Are you sure? I would certainly appreciate it."

"Yeah, no problem. I wanna hang out with her, anyway."

Mom smiles and kisses my cheek, again. "You're a gem. An absolute gem, you know that?"

"I think you might be biased."

"So what if I am? You have your licence on you?"

"Yep."

She slides the keys across the counter. "OK, thank you, sweetheart, and drive safe, OK?"

"Will do."

"And are you staying for dinner?" she asks.

"Am I invited?" I reply.

"You are always invited. I'll tell your father to throw another steak on the barbecue when he starts supper."

* * *

43

I sit in the Volvo in my old high school parking lot, feeling like a little bit of—OK a lot bit of—a creeper. Finally, I hear the bell which triggers six million memories, most of which are connected to Rylan. After a few minutes, kids start to swarm out and suddenly someone's knocking on the passenger door. I jump. Hell. It's Matilda. I unlock the door.

"You're not Mom," she offers, opening the passenger side door. I'm pretty sure that she sounds pretty glad to see me and that feels good.

"You caught me," I reply.

Matilda laughs, then asks, "So, what the hell are you doing here, little brother?" She's younger but taller, by a whole two centimetres or something.

"Meh," I answer non-committally. "You wanna go to McDick's or something?"

"Sbucks. And I'm driving. You look like shit."

I crawl over and sit hopelessly in the passenger seat.

Tilla climbs in beside me. She's not technically allowed to drive without someone over twenty-five in the car, because she's only an L driver (fucking BC driving rules—bane of every teenager's existence), but I really think she's making the safer choice at the moment. I don't say anything and she doesn't say anything back until we're through the drive-thru, drinks in hand and sitting on a concrete picnic bench near the strip mall.

"Nigh," she says. "*Nigh*." I suddenly zone back in.

"Huh? Sorry. What?"

"Are you going to tell me what the hell is going on?"

I shrug.

"Everyone OK?"

"Yeah."

"Shona and Rylan and DRIP and everyone?"

"Fine."

"OK. Mom and Dad are fine too, right?" Panic flares up slightly in her voice.

"Oh. God. Yeah, sorry, they're fine. So far as I know."

"Jesus, you had me freaked. So what's up?"

I take a drink. "Look, do you want to rent a movie or something?"

"You're seriously not going to tell me."

I don't answer her.

"You show up randomly at my school looking like microwaved shit and you're not even going to tell me what's wrong."

Yep, sounds about right.

"You are so frustrating, sometimes, Niles." She rolls her eyes. "But sure," she's humouring me, "let's rent some movies. By the way," she says as we climb back into the car, me feeling stable enough to drive somehow. "Nice neck. Violent, much? God, you and Rylan are practically cannibals."

I wish she'd stop saying his name.

* * *

Matilda and I sit on the couch in amicable silence. There's some movie that she chose playing, and I'm paying more attention to it than it warrants in hopes of tuning everything else out. Tilla's glancing over at me every few minutes, but I pretend to be so engrossed that I don't notice.

After about a half hour, we hear the garage door open and as it's shutting Dad and Kya come in. We shout hello and Kya races into the room. She's fresh from swimming lessons and smells like chlorine. I wrangle her into my arms and hoist her up onto my hip even though she typically considers herself too old for this sort of thing.

"What are YOU doing here?" she demands.

"Just thought I hadn't seen you in a while!" I answer brightly.

"You can fucking say that again!" she replies happily.

Matilda and I both stare at her. "What did you just say, Kya?" Til demands.

"I said, 'You can fuc—'"

"Well, how about you never say that again!" I cut her off. Christ, my seven-year-old sister cursing like, well, like my sixteen-year-old sister, who's gonna be in shit if our parents hear that.

"Why?" demands Kya.

"Because," I answer back.

Matilda gives me a look that absolutely says, "Honestly, you're useless." She kneels down, holding Kya by the shoulders and looks her straight in the eyes. "Because if you say that at school, you'll get a DT."

Kya's eyes get a little bigger and she lets out a low whistle. "I've never had a DT."

"I have," I say. "And they are AWFUL."

"How come?" she asks.

"I'm not talking about it," I reply, with a sinister undertone.

Kya looks appealingly to Matilda, who carries on in the same thread: "And if Mom and Dad hear you saying that, you'll be grounded."

"I've never been grounded either," Kya says solemnly.

"I have," Matilda says. "And I never want to be again."

"OK," Kya whispers. "Man, it's that bad, hey?"

"That bad," Matilda and I nod.

Matilda stares darkly back into Kya's eyes to affirm her point. Her expression shifts.

"Niles, come look at this," she says, her voice light, but hinting at worry.

"Look at what?" Kya demands, twisting around to look behind her.

"Kya-bear, don't move," Matilda says sweetly. Then to me, "Look at her eye." She taps her finger lightly underneath Kya's left eye. Kya squints.

"What?" she whines.

And I see it. A little part of her pupil is reflecting weirdly, almost like a cat's eye in the dark.

"Does your eye hurt, Kya-baby?" Matilda asks gently.

"No, but my shoulders do because you won't let go, Stupid!"

Matilda releases her and Kya races out of the room, her My Little Pony backpack being yanked along behind her.

We look at each other. "What is it?" I ask Matilda.

"I have no idea."

"Should we tell the parents?"

"Tell the parents what?" It's my father's voice. He sounds amused and he comes over to clap me on the shoulder.

"Indeed," Mom joins in, hugging me from behind and squooshing her cheek against mine.

At this point in time, Matilda would usually make a sarcastic, snotty remark about how Mom is never interested in hugging her, and that maybe if they'd let her move out they'd like her more, and then Mom would make a point of hugging Matilda, and Matilda would make a point of not responding. But not today.

"Have you seen Kya's eye?" Matilda asks hopefully, like maybe if Mom's already seen it then there's nothing to worry about.

"What do you mean?" Mom asks and I see Matilda's hope vanish.

"It's doing this weird reflecting thing. I don't know."

47

Mom's eyebrows crease. "I haven't noticed anything. Maybe it was just a reflection from the television. Which, Matilda, I do believe you're currently banned from for breaking curfew."

I hold my hand up in Matilda's defense. "My fault. I begged and pleaded."

I can tell Mom is going to let it slide, and Matilda looks at me gratefully.

Kya suddenly comes charging back into the room. "God, you guys are boring," she says matter-of-factly.

"Kya. Language," Mom warns automatically.

"Mom. Language," Kya mimics. God, Matilda and I would never have gotten away with that. I think child-rearing on the later side of middle age is a whole lot slacker.

My dad scoops Kya up by the armpits. She's wiry and kicks wildly, shrieking at him to put her down. Dad brings Kya's face close to his until they are having a staring contest, with her still suspended in the air.

"Charlotte, honey, I think you should take a look at this," he says calmly. He places Kya's feet back on the floor.

Mom tilts Kya's face up towards her own, and looks at the offending eye intently. Kya stills, seems to finally get that something is going on.

"I'll go give the nurses' hotline a call," Mom says quietly, and heads for the kitchen.

"What?" Kya asks.

No one answers her.

"What?!" she repeats louder, impatiently.

"Nothing!" Matilda says brightly. "Niles and I were just thinking that maaaaybe you'd like to go mini-golfing tonight." Matilda looks at Dad who nods his confirmation before turning and leaving the room.

"For serious?" asks Kya.

We nod.

"Heck, yeah I would!" she screeches.

* * *

Mom says the nurse won't say anything definite, but she said to make an appointment with our family doctor first thing in the morning. She pulls out her laptop and types rapidly, researching. Her mouth flattens into a tight, thin line and she claps her computer shut. She says no one is going to worry about anything until we know something for sure. So of course, we all worry—except Kya.

Kya doesn't question why she's allowed to go mini-golfing on a school night. She doesn't get why Dad unhesitatingly makes her a grilled cheese when she complains about the chicken. She is thrilled when she's allowed to stay up late that night watching movies she doesn't really understand but is trying to watch anyway because she wants Matilda and me to think she's smart. And she doesn't get why Rylan isn't here. When it's getting late and she's getting tired and cranky, she tells me he's more fun than me anyway, and that I'm stupid for not inviting him over. Matilda glances over at me worriedly, thinking that that, after everything today, will upset me. It doesn't. It seems pretty trivial in comparison.

"Come on, Kya, this movie is lame," Matilda says. "If you go to bed now, I'll do your hair up in a billion little braids for tomorrow."

"Promise?"

"Promise," Matilda confirms.

"Deal." Kya solemnly sticks out her hand and Tilla shakes it.

When she comes back down a half hour later, Tilla folds up next to me on the couch.

"Do you think it's really something?" she asks.

"I don't know," I answer, truthfully.

"I looked at the stuff Mom was Googling. There's like…kid cataracts and stuff."

"Yeah, but it's probably nothing serious."

"Yeah, but it could be."

Yup. It really could be. I wrap an arm around Matilda's shoulder and rest my head on hers as she slumps against my arm.

"They'll figure it out," I promise.

"They'd better," she whispers.

- 6 -

After Kya and our parents are asleep, or at least have gone to bed, without anyone bothering to say anything to Matilda about having school in the morning (for once), she and I drive to my place to get some clothes and stuff, because I have a feeling I might want to be home with everyone for at least a couple of days. In the car, she picks the music. We quietly mumble along to the verses and sing along to the choruses: a prime strategy when one has nothing pleasant to talk about.

When we get back to the house we crash in my old bedroom for a little bit, neither one of us wanting to be alone. I don't know why exactly, but Matilda seems way older than she is. She still sometimes acts like a brat and picks fights with Mom, but sometimes I wonder if it's because she's actually pissed or because she thinks that's what teenagers do. Either way, I'm not sure our parents give her enough credit. It's weird, but growing up—if I was in a particularly morbid mood—I'd think about what would have happened if our parents died, and for some reason I always just assumed that Matilda would keep Kya and me in line—which realistically, is completely irrational. I mean, I'm three years older. Guess it's the whole girls have a higher emotional maturity level, or whatever.

I almost tell her about Rylan, but then I realize to do that I'd have to go into the details of my sex life, and mature or not, she's still my sister, and I do not have any inclination whatsoever to know the status of her hymen or, maybe, lack thereof, so, assuming she'd feel similarly, and having thoroughly grossed myself out, I leave it alone.

Finally, Matilda drags herself off to bed. I get undressed, and when I do, the condom falls out of my pocket. Shit. What the fuck am I supposed to do? I'm no good at this. Hell, I still have all four grandparents: I've never lost a single person in my entire life. I've never...done anything, felt anything of magnitude. So far my existence has been completely devoid of tragedy. And I guess now I'm paying for the nineteen years of...luck. Or something. Like no one should be happy for that long. But the fact that it's Kya who will maybe be paying for it —well, that karma's just fucked.

Rylan hasn't called. Or texted. Well, he never texts. He thinks texting is lazy and a waste of time. If you want to talk, pick up the phone and dial, is his philosophy.

Fuck. I really hope this—everything, Rylan and Kya and—I just hope it isn't anything. I just want to sleep. So that it will go away. I'm obviously really good at dealing with shit.

* * *

I sleep in for hours, having already decided not to bother with class today. I don't actually get up until noon, when my phone starts vibrating from the floor.

It probably makes me an asshole that I'm disappointed that it's Shona. OK, I'm not disappointed that it's Shona; I'm just disappointed that it's not Rylan.

"Let me tell you a fun story," she starts in as soon as I pick up. "When, say, Person A tells Person B, who, by the way, is their BEST FRIEND, to call them, and then they don't, Person B gets bitchy and a little concerned."

"Sorry, Shone."

"Better be." She forgives me instantly. "What's up?"

I tell her what's going on with Kya.

"Well, now I feel like a selfish bitch. I'm so sorry, Niles."

"Yeah." Because what else can she say, right? Of course she says she's sorry and it's probably not anything and all that, but...honestly. There's nothing you can say.

"When do you find out for sure?"

"I think the appointment's this afternoon. I guess they'll be home in a couple of hours."

"Where are they now?"

"You know my mom. Ten bucks says Kya was frogmarched to school right up until the appointment."

"Well, that's probably good, right? Keep things normal?"

I sigh, I guess she's right. "Yeah."

"How's Rylan taking it? He loves that kid."

"...Fine," I find myself saying. I don't have the energy to deal with that issue too, not with Shona. I can barely deal with it myself. Whatever *it* actually is.

"Ha. Fine, I bet. Let me tell you, Nigh, it's all an act. Ten to one says he's only being fine for your sake. Not that I necessarily want him anywhere near you right now."

"Yeah, well..."

I tell her I have to go, and she says to call her later when I know what's going on and I tell her I will.

I shower and putz around the kitchen, make myself some eggs and then clean the kitchen for my parents. I'm halfway through vacuuming the floor when Matilda shows up.

"Shouldn't you be at school?" I ask automatically.

"Spare block and then photography, which I have this niggling feeling that I won't fail if I skip once. Besides..."

She doesn't have to finish, just shrugs and I get it. I can't concentrate either.

"Wanna play, like, Checkers or something?" she asks half desperately.

* * *

Mom doesn't come home for hours. Dad calls and tells us that Kya's been referred to a specialist and they are all heading there for an urgent consult.

By the time they get home my mom is just barely holding it together. Kya however, seems unfazed, whizzing upstairs, and within seconds we have Pearl Jam blaring down the stairs. Please do not ask me why my seven-year-old sister listens to Pearl Jam, and only Pearl Jam, because it is one of life's great mysteries, which I have long since given up trying to solve.

"Kya, shut your door!" my mom pleads. For a moment nothing happens, but then thankfully the music is muffled.

Til and I are standing practically at attention.

"Well?" Matilda urges.

"The. Um. The ophthalmologist thinks—is almost certain that it's—God, I can't even pronounce it. Retina-blasty something."

We stare at her blankly.

"Cancer."

Jesus. I didn't expect that. Why didn't I expect that? Everyone gets fucking cancer. Matilda moves close to me, her elbow practically digging into my ribs.

"Where's Dad?" Matilda asks.

"He's in the car. He needs a minute."

Shit shit shit shit shit. I need to fix this. I can't fix this, I want to fix this, but...I don't even know what happens now.

"What...what happens next? A...biopsy or something?" I'm trying to rationalize this. Or I'm begging, I can't even tell.

"In her *eye*?" Matilda hisses.

"No. No..." Mom tells us. "No biopsy. An MRI. But that will take a couple weeks. And it will tell us if it's spread..."

"No," I refuse. This is not happening. No fucking way.

"And then what?" we demand.

54

"It all depends. If it's spread, chemo. If it stays in one...they'll most likely—" She cuts herself off with a soft sob.

"They'll what?"

She's shaking. Matilda moves to her, hugging her like she probably hasn't done in years.

"They'll cut out my baby's eye."

Matilda and my mom cling to each other. I stand uselessly nearby, drowning.

* * *

We all stagnate while we wait. I drag myself to class, spend a bit of time with Shona, and then go straight home to my parents' place afterwards, to spend as much time as I possibly can with Kya. I try to think of every fun thing I can think of and hate myself for not having been around her more since I moved out.

Kya doesn't get it. Mom has tried to explain it to her, but she can't bring herself to tell Kya that they might have to...Fuck. How do you tell a kid something like that?

There's a cancellation and Kya gets her MRI within the week. It confirms the cancer, which is currently contained. It should be cause for a celebration but mostly I just feel like I accidentally ate a pound of lead. They are sending Kya to the children's hospital in Vancouver for treatment. Mom, thankfully, does mostly freelance editing and so she can take time off work to go with her. She has a university friend she can stay with there, and Dad will go over on his days off.

The night before they leave we have a big family dinner together and Matilda and I bake Kya a cake, and she tells us we're weird because it's not her birthday. In the morning we all drive out to the ferry terminal to see them off and my dad stands at the departure bay for a good fifteen minutes, just

55

watching the *Spirit of British Columbia* shrink into the distance.

"Maybe they'll see some whales. Kya's always bitching about how she never sees any whales," Matilda mentions, finally.

"Maybe they will," my dad agrees.

We get back into the car and head home, a whole, useless Saturday flopping before us.

* * *

Dad sits silently in the living room all afternoon, and we know better than to disturb him. One of his friends from down the street calls him around four, and then Dad leaves, saying he'll be back late. My dad rarely drinks. Tonight, I expect, he'll come home hammered. I get that.

Matilda and I go for a run by the water and then grab some ice cream. It's spring and the cherry blossoms are coming out. It's ungodly beautiful and we're plain old sad.

Later, Til's friend Courtney calls, and I can see Matilda assessing me from the corner of her eye. I don't blame her for wanting to get the fuck out of this house where she can get some actual sympathy instead of just caring for my broken-down ass all day.

"Look, Court," I hear her saying from the kitchen, "I can't tonight. Tomorrow, though? I miss you like crazy and I need some time to just..." She pauses as Courtney speaks, then resumes, "Yeah. Exactly. I'll call you in the morning and we'll meet at the mall or something, shop or something? Yeah." They end the conversation and she comes back into the living room.

"Nigh?" she says after we've sat together for another one of those long periods of silence which seem to have been consuming us for the last couple of days.

"Yeah?"

"I know you're trying to be the stoic older brother and all."

This catches me off-guard. I've been feeling like the shitty older brother who can't seem to offer even the semblance of comfort to his far more mature and capable younger sister.

"But...look, why don't you just call Rylan, invite him over, let him take care of you, you know?"

I don't know how to reply.

"What?" she says. She gets up and walks to the kitchen. She comes back holding the house phone. "Look. Here. Phone. Don't worry, it'll be fine. I looked it up on the internet: kids with eye cancer have, like a ninety percent survival rate, especially if it's caught early, so, it's fine. I'm fine. You don't need to bum around here taking care of me. Why don't you let him come over and take care of you for a little while. Go on. Dial."

The phone sits uselessly in my palm.

"Niles," she says, prodding me. "Call your boyfriend!"

I finally find my voice. "I can't."

"Whaddaya mean you...Holy fuck." She shakes her head at me. "Holy FUCK. What did you do?"

I take offense to that, or I feel I should, at any rate, "What do you mean, what did *I* do?"

"Did you fucking dump him? Is that what you were all...you know, about? Holy fuck, why the fuck would you do that?"

"I didn't fucking dump him!" I defend myself.

"Well, I somehow doubt he dumped you!" she retorts fiercely.

"How the fuck do you know?" I demand.

"Oh, come on! We both know Rylan's fucking crazy about you. He'd never leave you. Unless you told him to."

"Oh, we both know that, do we?" I explode. "What the actual fuck, Matilda? This is one thing you don't know shit about."

I'm being hurtful. Goddamn it. I don't want to be a fucking asshole, I just—why is she saying this shit?

"Fine," she says, breath coming heavy, but siphoned between her teeth at the same time. "Give me the phone."

Relieved, I pass the receiver to her.

And she fucking dials.

I hear Rylan answer after one ring, but I can't discern his tone of voice. "Niles?" God. I miss him so much. Insurmountably much.

Til glares at me, then, speaking sweetly into the phone, "Actually, Rylan, this is Matilda speaking—"

She stalks into the kitchen where she keeps her voice low on purpose so that I can't hear what she's saying. A few minutes later she rejoins me.

"He'll be on the next bus over," she says. And I swear she sounds almost smug.

- 7 -

He knocks. My mom always tells him that he can come on in, that he doesn't need to knock, he's family, and he always replies, "But you have a knocker!" Like the novelty never wears off.

I don't move.

Matilda looks at me. I just sit there. She gets up to answer it. I watch them through the doorway of the living room.

"Tilla," Rylan says before hugging her.

I stand up nervously. I don't know what to do with my body. My hands are dangling awkwardly. I shove them in my pockets, and then take them out again.

Ry and Tilla are talking quietly at the door, still. I can't quite make out what they are saying. He's got his hand on her upper arm, and they are leaning in towards each other. Sometimes I feel like everyone else in my family knows how to relate to him better than I do. In high school, he came on family trips with us. He's spent Christmases at our house. Before I moved out he was practically a permanent fixture here. He just fits. And I...

I'm just so frickin' glad he's here.

But I still don't know what to do with myself.

Til heads into the kitchen. Rylan walks through the front hall, towards me, looking straight at me. I can't move.

He doesn't stop or slow down until he reaches me. He doesn't hesitate for a single second, just wraps his arms tight around my body.

I can't compute this. We don't hug. Well, outside of sex, though that usually isn't hugging so much as...grasping. And we tend to cuddle during movies, so I guess that's pretty similar, and sometimes when we're out together, he'll throw an arm around my shoulder, but we never just...hug. I mean, he hugs my sisters, and my parents, but we don't. I don't know how to react. He's got one arm under one of mine, and the other over top of my shoulder. Typical hug mechanics, except that my arms are still hanging pathetic and inactive at my sides, which is ridiculous because I finally have something to do with them. So, tentatively, I hug him, you know, back.

He holds me tighter and I hold him tighter, burying my head in his hoodie because he is here. With me. When everything is so shitty and we don't know what's going to happen to Kya or when, and he had every right to say, "Well, gee whiz, that's too bad...not my problem," because I'm such an idiot and went and fucked everything up, but he didn't say that. Instead he came right over and walked into my living room and is hugging me. Because Kya's sick and we don't have any of the answers.

I find myself lodging my teeth into his shoulder. My eyes are all prickling and stuff, but I haven't cried since I was probably like eight, so I don't know if I'm the type of person who cries, even if they feel like it. I just am not sure I really remember how to, so instead I'm biting him, and pressing my fist into his back, hard, and he just keeps on holding me and letting me hurt him even though I know I should stop and I just can't.

My eyes are tightly closed because that somehow makes me feel like I'm a little further away from this whole situation with everything than I am, so I don't see Matilda coming back into the room; I don't know she's there until Rylan whispers into my hair, "Nigh, baby, I think you might be starting to freak your sister out..."

My eyes fly open both at his words and the pet name which he has never even once called me before and I see Matilda standing beside us, looking at me like she's kind of worried I'm going to dissolve entirely.

I extract my teeth from Rylan's shoulder and slowly relax the hug, even if I don't really want to. He runs a hand over the back of my head, and kisses my temple before pulling me down, half on top of him, on the couch.

"The movie's your choice tonight, Miss Attila," he says, sprawling out behind me on the couch. Matilda shuffles through some DVDs.

"Any suggestions?" she asks.

"Something that doesn't require us to think," he answers. His arms snakes around my abs, pulling me back into him. He kisses the back of my neck quickly. "You OK, liebling?" he whispers—another remnant from his high school German endeavour. He doesn't call me it hardly ever, though. I nod. I'm OK enough. He exhales into my hair, and then shifts himself a little bit higher so that he can see the screen. I'm a mess and I'm exhausted and all I can feel is Rylan, steady and warm behind me.

My phone rings. I don't respond, so Rylan reaches into my pocket and takes it out and answers it.

"Hey, Shona," he says quietly.

"So, you're not Niles," I hear her reply.

"You wanna talk?" he asks me. I shake my head. I do not have that kind of energy.

"He's OK," Rylan tells her, "but he'll call you tomorrow, alright?"

"He's right there next to you, isn't he?" Shona accuses.

"Yep."

"Well, I wouldn't want to interfere with your spoon sesh," Shona resigns, peaceably.

"You're a peach."

"Give him a kiss for me, yeah?"

Rylan kisses my ear. "Done."

"Thanks. LOVE YOU, NILES," Shona half-yells.

Rylan holds the phone to my mouth. "Love you," I reply.

"Night, Shona," Ry says, bringing the phone back to his ear.

"Night, Rylan. Take good care of our boy, you get me?"

"I gotcha," Rylan answers. He ends the call and slides my phone back into my pocket, absently rubbing circles over my side and abdomen with his palm until I'm as good as asleep.

Even though it's not (even close), he does a pretty damn good job of convincing me everything's OK.

* * *

We stay awake hiding in the TV until I'm headachey with exhaustion.

"C'mon," says Rylan, finally. He worms his way out from behind me and flicks off the TV and stands over me, waiting. He offers his hands and I take them, letting him pull me up until we're level. I don't feel entirely planted because for a minute we're just standing there, like, holding hands and looking at each other and I don't think we've ever done that before and so I don't think I know how. Rylan seems to, though, and he smiles softly, squeezes my hands and gently bumps our fists up against my thighs and kisses me. Lightly, ridiculously lightly, before releasing one of my hands and pulling me along upstairs to my old room, where I strip off my jeans and shirt, brush my teeth. He waits patiently for my toothbrush, and when I'm done I hand it to him and go and sit on the side of the bed. I watch him floss in the bathroom across the hall.

When Rylan returns to the bedroom he starts undressing, unself-consciously. He foots the door closed and sits beside me and I still don't know what I'm supposed to do. We spent a million hours together in this bed in high school: skipped periods and late nights and Saturday afternoons, like we could never get enough. I guess we couldn't, because we're still doing that. It's just...him and me and this bed only ever equate to sex.

Exhaustion wins and I crawl gracelessly under the quilt and top sheet and curl in on myself. Rylan follows suit, sliding up behind me and slipping his arm underneath mine and pressing his palm to my chest. I exhale a long, shaky breath.

"What are you doing?" he asks me, and I know he's really asking what's wrong, but that's too deep a territory with us. I lean helplessly back into him, knowing I shouldn't, knowing stuff isn't sorted and we're not OK like we're pretending. Rylan nuzzles the side of my face with his, the roughness of his stubble familiar and soothing.

He squeezes my body tighter against him, into him, and even if he's not doing anything to turn me on, I'm afraid at any second he might try and that thought honestly disgusts me, because I don't want it, not even at all.

"I don't want to have sex right now," tumbles out of my mouth before I even know it's there and I cannot believe I did that—that I just fucking *acknowledged* it and with it...everything. Shit. Holy shit. My pulse spikes with terror and fuck I—God, I should have just let him fuck me and then he could have left and then I would've known that he'd come back, probably. Fuck...I...

"What the hell, Nigh?" He smashes through my thoughts. I don't know what to expect. Like, is he going to deny the whole last three years, pretend not to know what I'm talking about?

63

Or maybe he'll just up and leave: strip my body of his and take off and I'll be here, alone, again, because I had to go and fucking open my stupid, shitty mouth. He's still talking but I can barely bring myself to listen because I know whatever he's going to say is probably the last fucking thing he'll ever say to me, holy shit, I'm fucking hysterical. Holy shit...

"Seriously, just how much of an asshole do you think I am?" His voice is incredulous or—hurt? He doesn't pull away, just maybe holds me tighter in place, which makes me feel safe even though I know I can't be and nothing makes any sense right now. "Shit," he whispers.

He still doesn't let me go and yet I'm still waiting for him to leave: to get up and walk out of the door and silently proclaim the nothing we have officially over.

Instead, he's...he's kissing my face and I don't know what is going on because I *told* him I don't want to have sex right now. I *just told* him that, so what the fuck is he doing? I never once thought he'd force it; I swore to Shona up and down a thousand times over that he'd never force it: that there's rough, and then there's something else entirely. I can't believe this. He's still kissing me when I don't want to do anything like that, not tonight, Jesus, not now.

My neck cranes to look at him, to get him to stop somehow, but instead he fucking kisses my lips, he's got his hands on my face and his mouth over mine, and I can't take it, I seriously can't. I told him I didn't want...I have never used my size against him, but I fucking do now. I turn halfway around and press my hands into his shoulders, and he keeps on fucking kissing me, so I shove him, as hard as I can, and he fires backwards into the wall the bed is pushed up against.

"I said I don't want to have sex right now!" I almost scream but stop myself—I don't want Matilda to come barging in here—so it comes out strangled-sounding instead.

64

Rylan stares at me from the far side of the bed, eyebrows and face screwed up in wonder, probably disbelieving that I would ever say no to him, the bastard. He shakes his head and sets his jaw. He sits up slowly and leans against the wall, brows furrowed and lips thin.

He makes no move to touch me and I'm so fucking relieved. Instead, calmly, carefully he says, "Niles. Baby. I don't want to have sex with you right now, either."

He's doing that thing where he looks me straight in the eyes, not letting me look away. And, finally—*finally*—I get it. I get that maybe I've had this whole thing wrong from the start. That things are kind of fucked right now, and Rylan can maybe be an asshole sometimes, but he's here, and that should be a big fucking clue, because no matter where things stand with me, he loves Kya and suddenly I'm sure she's all he's been thinking of, same as me. I cover my face with my palms and press my fingers desperately into my forehead because I might sort of get it but that doesn't mean I know what comes next.

"OK," I find myself murmuring. "Yeah, OK. Yeah. I get it, I just. Fuck. Can you please just—what *do* you want?" It comes out in what could be interpreted as a whimper and I feel my skin flush in embarrassment.

"Lie down," he directs (and I'm so, so relieved to be released from decision-making duty), "and stop acting like a crazy person."

I tentatively lie back down, facing the ceiling. He leans over me, one hand on either side of my body.

"I just wanna fucking...comfort you," he whispers, "but you've got to let me, OK?"

I clench close my eyes and nod and for the second time tonight I just feel like crying. His fingers trace my jaw and slowly ease the tension from my body. Finally, he pulls away, lying down beside me.

For long minutes we stay like that, lying there, not touching and not sleeping either. He's restless. I can hear and feel him shuffling around, then pausing, and then rolling over again. And then suddenly, he pulls me over on top of him, faceplanting me into his chest, my knees curling into his calves. His arms vine around my waist and back and I feel his breath in my hair.

"Is this OK?" he whispers. And I nod frantically because yes, God yes, fuck yes, I need this.

It dawns on me that I like this, this being close to him with no expectations, no time limits or imminent destination. It's all peaceful and unfamiliar. I don't want to ruin this, but at the same time I can't foresee myself ever getting another chance. I force myself to speak.

"Should we...talk?" I ask, quietly.

"Do you seriously want to go into all our shit right now?" he replies earnestly. "Like we can, I mean, I absolutely will, but we're tired and—do you want to, honestly?" I shake my head, unequivocally relieved, because I realize I don't want to talk things out. I mean, I do. But not now, not when I feel like a sudden movement could dissolve me into splinters. "We will though," Rylan promises, as if reading my thoughts, "and soon, OK?"

"Yeah," I agree. "Soon."

Rylan sighs softly, his palm running up and down my back, slow and constant.

"What are you doing?" I ask, half by accident and unable to stop myself. "We don't *do* this."

"Yeah," he replies, "well, maybe we should."

I find myself nodding into his chest again, and I allow one arm to creep around under his arm and over his shoulder. He temporarily tightens his hold on me, and, for the second time tonight, I think we're hugging.

"See?" he says lightly into my hair. "Don't ever think that I don't know what's best for you."

I can't tell if he's joking, and for some reason I find that that doesn't matter. I now have complete evidence that I'm all kinds of fucked up, because somehow, that sentiment honestly comforts me.

- 8 -

Of course, he's gone in the morning. He doesn't leave a note or a little bouquet of wildflowers, or coffee and a muffin on my bedside table like (just maybe) a part of my brain half-wishes he would—not because I crave flowers or muffins, but because I do crave reassurance. He does, however, change my laptop desktop to a Paint document: his mouse-messy scrawl (and that's pretty messy), saying, "AT WORK EARNING FUNDS FOR A VANCOUVER TRIP NEXT WEEKEND, YEAH? CALL YOU SOON." And a picture of what might be a heart. Or a penis. It's hard to tell.

Rylan works at a pet store, Nook, except that's it's not like, cats and dogs and bunnies, so it doesn't stink. The only pets Nook sells are aquarium dwellers, mostly tropical fish. Rylan is mainly a very, like, stereotypically cool guy: he's like the kind of guy who leans against walls and railings and smokes and looks aloof (except that he doesn't actually smoke), and everyone around just looks at him and goes, "Fuck, that is one cool guy." But all the coolness Rylan projects is utterly undone by one simple fact: he's a fish geek. An intense one. Like...if he could not come home from work, sometimes I think he might sleep there. Yeah. He really likes those fish.

* * *

He does call later and of course, we don't talk, not about anything relating to anything, at any rate. He tells me about Mr. Murdoch, the Swiss guy who comes in to watch the

69

lobsters shed their shells. I tell him about my morning. Getting up, showering, eating. I have nothing exciting to report, but hey, he asked. He tells me his break is over and he's gotta run. He says he'll come over after his shift.

And that's our week. He spends the night. He holds me while we sleep and in the morning he leaves for work. He phones me on his break, heads over after dinner. We don't talk. Well, we talk, but we don't, you know, *talk*. I think about it and I can tell he thinks about it but neither of us says anything, me because I'm back to square one (namely: being terrified of losing him, possibly even more so than I was before, because now I've seen him like this—how he's been all week) and him because, maybe, I'm not too sure, but because maybe he's worried I'm too fragile or something. Maybe I'm worried about that, too.

* * *

We don't go to Vancouver that weekend because I have a sociology essay I can't get any more extensions on and Rylan has to cover a shift at Nook. I sit around my parents' mostly empty house all day, procrastinating on my essay, watching bad TV and eating Corn Pops.

I hate Corn Pops. Kya and Rylan love them.

* * *

Another week and I actually get assignments done and stuff so that Rylan and I can go visit Kya for sure. I miss her, which doesn't make sense because I never came home much to see her since I moved out. Feeling pretty guilty about that now, actually. Dad and Matilda ended up going last weekend, and they said Kya's as wilful as ever, and every time I've talked to her on the phone, she sounds that way, but it will be good to see her and Mom with my own eyes or whatever.

Rylan shows up around seven-thirty Saturday morning. He passes me a double-double, while he sucks back his English toffee cappuccino. Which is totally not at all a cappuccino and one of the many reasons I hate that drink. That doesn't mean that I don't like the way it tastes when he leans in and kisses me. I'm not sure if it's a good thing that I'm getting used to this: him kissing me without it leading anywhere intense. We've been doing more of it in the last two weeks than we have in the last three years. I mean, before, we kissed a lot, but we also had *a lot* of sex, so chances are the kissing would lead up to it.

We still haven't actually had sex, not since before the misery-inducing Condom Incident. I sometimes catch myself wondering if we ever will again. I mean, the kissing leads me to believe that we probably will, that we're just waiting out the worrying over Kya first, but sometimes I wonder that maybe if Kya gets better then Rylan will take off. Which, Shona informs me, is one fuck of a stupid attitude. And it's not like I don't know I'm being paranoid and irrational, but strangely knowing I'm being paranoid and irrational does not actually stop me from being paranoid and irrational.

"You OK?" Rylan asks, lips too close to mine for us to have a real conversation.

"Yeah," I reply, barely actually making any noise.

He kisses me again once we climb in the car. He doesn't actually have his licence but he drives anyway, even if it is my parents' car and if we're in an accident the insurance and legal shit will be a veritable nightmare. But I'm not up to it and he somehow knows it.

"Do you wanna stop and grab something for The Monster?" he asks. He means Kya. Sometimes he calls her Kya-Monster and she loves it, mainly by pretending to hate it.

"Let's get her something when we get there."

"We?" Rylan asks, his voice teasing. "*I* already got her something." He motions to his duffel bag in the backseat. I twist awkwardly to reach behind us and finally manage to get the zipper open. On top of everything is what feels like a book. I tug it loose. He flicks on the overhead light because it's not actually light out yet.

"It's dangerous to drive like that," I inform him, inanely.

"Well, what do you think?" he asks, gesturing towards the book, and ignoring my statement.

It's a book on sharks. As I leaf through I realize it's not your typical shark book, like migratory patterns or something like that. No, this is about shark attacks. It's full of bloody photographs and diagrams of toothy jaws and survivors' stories and grotesque pictures of recently mauled bodies. In most kids, I'd say it would definitely cause nightmares. But not Kya.

"She'll love it," I tell him, turning to a page inventorying items found in dead sharks' stomachs.

"I know," he agrees smugly.

And of course he's right.

* * *

That afternoon when she sees it, she practically hoots with joy.

"DID YOU SEE THIS?" she demands, revealing a particularly bloody photograph to us in her small, bright hospital room. Quite frankly, it's making the teddy bear I bought at the gift shop look seriously lame.

72

Rylan grins. "Tell you what, Kya. How do you wanna see a shark in real life?"

She looks at him suspiciously. "Like on TV, you mean?"

"No..." he says, his voice conspiratorial. "Like at the aquarium..."

I see what he's doing: feeding his own fish addiction under the façade of entertaining my younger sister. He catches me rolling my eyes and keeps on grinning.

"Seriously?" Kya asks, still looking for the trick ending.

"Seriously. Even ask Niles."

"Seriously, Niles? Can we?"

I shrug. "If it's alright with Mom."

"HELL, YEAH!" Kya shrieks and rushes out the door in search of permission.

Of course, Mom is more than happy to let us take Kya off of her hands for the day. She looks tired, and I suspect she is. Kya, even when hospitalized (it turns out), is a pit of crackling energy, and I know by the end of today I'm going to be exhausted, at the very least. Before we even get to the car, I stop Kya and search her eyes: her surgery is scheduled the day after tomorrow and it's weird knowing that after this weekend I won't ever look her in both eyes again.

"Stop it!" Kya squirms away. "All anyone ever does is look at my stupid eye. I wish they'd just cut it out already!"

We load her into the car. I feel a bit more up to driving so I play chauffeur: Rylan sits in the backseat changing the words of generic kids' songs into run-on poop jokes and sending Kya into convulsions of laughter.

At the aquarium I get side-tracked by the brain sponges. I've liked them ever since I was a kid and there's not a crowd around the glass like there is elsewhere.

"What are you looking at *plants* for?" Kya demands.

73

Before I can answer, Rylan cuts in, "Believe me, Kya-Monster, you'll never understand him."

Kya rolls her eyes. "You mean he's a giant weirdo. Let's go!"

She drags him on ahead to the stingray tank. Is it odd that I feel like a third wheel when hanging out with my boyfriend and my seven-year-old sister? Probably. But I don't really mind it. I'm just kinda glad they have each other.

Eventually we end up outside the beluga tank. It's a school day and too early in the year for too-too many tourists. Rylan and I sit down, our thighs touching with just enough pressure to be more than accidental, and allow Kya to climb around on the stone bleachers. This apparently grows boring, because soon she's climbing up Rylan's back, perching on his shoulders like a bird that doesn't know it's too big for the power line.

Besides the brain sponges, the belugas are my favourite. Even though I'm sure, compared to, you know, the ocean, the tank they are in is pathetically small, for some reason they seem so satisfied with life, like swimming in endless circles is a perfectly decent way to spend a lifetime. Maybe they're right.

"The belugas in Washington did tricks," Kya tells us—the last zoo she went to was with my parents in Seattle and Tacoma.

"Well, maybe these belugas aren't into that sort of thing," Rylan offers.

"There were walruses there, too," she continues, leaning over the top of Rylan's head and using her fingers to mush up his face. She grabs onto his lips, pressing them together and pulling them outwards, effectively inhibiting his capability for speech. I can't think of much to say either, but Kya feels the need to continue. "Ever seen a walrus' thingy?"

I almost choke, and I'm not even eating anything.

"KYA!" I exclaim, but Rylan, now that Kya's moved on to prodding at his cheeks, interrupts, obviously entertained.

"Can't say that I have."

"Ginormous," Kya informs us, matter-of-factly.

"Jesus, Kya. Can we please talk about something else?" I say firmly, and I can feel myself blushing. It's not like I'm a prude, but I'm trying not to actively encourage her, for my poor mother's sake. Rylan's imploding with withheld laughter.

"Why?" she asks.

"Because one day you'll be in company where bringing up the size, or even the existence, of walrus' 'thingies' just won't be appropriate."

She sighs discontentedly.

"Hey, why don't you tell us about how things are at the hospital?" I encourage.

She drapes her arms around Rylan's neck and presses her cheek against the top of his head, looking at me.

"They're OK."

"OK. How?"

"Jeez! I don't know? Just OK!"

"Well, what do you do? Are there other kids?"

"Niles. It's a *children's* hospital," Kya tells me, irritably.

"Right." I'm an idiot. "Well, do you like them?"

"Most of them."

"Do you guys...play?"

"I guess."

I'm done. I've got nothing. I look at Rylan.

"Any crush-worthy kids?" he asks, and of course Kya looks delighted.

"Maaaaaybe."

"Ooooh, really, Miss Monster? Do tell."

"Well," Kya says, and her voice goes kind of hushed. This is absurd. She's seven. She's in, what? The second grade? Kids don't get crushes in the second grade. Do they? Did I have a crush in the second grade? I don't know if I ever had crushes. I

75

don't remember liking girls. Or anyone, really. Like there was a vague feeling of supposed to be feeling things for girls and then there was kind of thinking about sex, and a general sense and mostly having that do it for me, and then there was Rylan. So I'm pretty much positive that I didn't know who or what I wanted when I was in the second grade. But fuck it, Rylan probably did. He's probably known his entire life that he's wanted a submissive...cum slut. Fuck. I am so not thinking about this right now.

"Well what!" Rylan prods.

"Welllll." Kya looks thoughtful, which is weird, because I think I've only seen Kya look thoughtful about once in her life, and that was when I asked her what she wanted for Christmas and she was trying to choose between a Transformers piñata and an electric blue cover for her iPod. "He's really sick."

That gets me.

"What do you mean?" Rylan's voice has softened.

"Well, we don't hang out much, because he gets tired a lot...but he's high-lar-ious. He's really cool, too. He takes Post-Its and he draws stickmen on them, and then when you flip through them, it looks like the stickmen are moving and they are so funny, and on one he even had a guy water-ski into a cliff." She giggles uproariously. "And this other guy went hot-air-ballooning into a stealth bomber."

"Sounds...morbid," Rylan says. I'm still trying to figure out how Kya knows what a stealth bomber is.

"He says he's probably going to die."

Well...shit, son. Kya tells us so calmly, and I don't get it. How can she just accept that, when the very thought freaks me the fuck out?

"He told you that?" Rylan asks quietly.

"Yeah. One day. He was really tired. And he had to have chemo, but now he doesn't anymore."

"What do you say to that?" I ask, not really meaning to say it out loud.

"I told him he was full of shit," she tells me, matter-of-factly.

"Oh." I don't exactly have a reply.

"I don't want chemo," Kya says after a while. "Cole says it sucks."

"Cole," Rylan repeats. "Is that his name?"

"Yup." Another pause, and then, "I'm probably in love with him."

It's all I can do to keep from snorting.

"Oh really?" Rylan asks, his voice slightly teasing.

"Yeah," Kya answers, like it's no big thing, which, given that she's seven, it probably isn't. Except that given the situation, it is. "He said it helps. To have people who love you around. So I figured if I'm going to be around him I should love him."

"Makes sense," Rylan nods.

"You love me?" Kya half-orders.

"Oodles!" Rylan answers, pulling her by the armpits over his head in some sort of awkward somersault until she's sprawled in his lap and he's holding her tightly.

"And you love....Matilda?" she prompts.

"You bet," he responds easily.

"Any my mom and dad?" Oh shit. I know where this is going. I shift away so that Rylan's leg isn't touching mine anymore.

"Of course," he replies.

"Annnnnnnnd NILES?" she crows.

And I swear he's not going to say a word. We're going to sit together in this horrible silence for the rest of our lives, which won't be very long, because I intend on drowning both Kya and myself in the beluga tank, stat.

But before I get a chance to hurtle us over the plexi-glass, Rylan's hand somehow seeks me out, hooking over the top of my thigh, forcing our legs back into contact.

"More than anything," he tells her. Or...me?

I can't move, closer or away. Or blink. Or swallow.

And so...I guess what this is, is proof.

I don't know a single fucking thing about anything.

- 9 -

Finally, after McDonald's French fries dipped in McDonald's soft serve and another couple of hours of Kya introducing us to every single person she's ever met in the hospital, she releases us. We don't say much on the ride back to the hotel, too exhausted to manipulate sentences.

When we get in the door we both just pass out on the bed. It's one of those things where for the first five minutes you promise yourself you'll get up and do something in just a couple of minutes. But when those couple of minutes pass, you still can't move, so you give yourself permission to just sleep and so I don't know how long I've been asleep when Rylan wakes me up.

I can't tell if it's a dream or not at first. Rylan's straddling me, fingers clamped onto my shoulders, teeth leaving sharp nips up and down my neck. When the pain finally registers as overly real for a dream state, I open my eyes and he grins and latches his mouth onto mine. His kissing seems to give way to tongue fucking almost immediately, tongue stud beating against the roof of my mouth, my teeth.

Without removing his mouth, he unbuttons and yanks off my sweater; his hands then assume their position, digging fiercely into my skin. He rolls his hips, grinding his clothed dick against mine, which willingly responds. He bites at my lips, which are still trying almost pathetically to kiss him back. He manoeuvres his hands again, one twisted in my hair, pulling, the other teasing my nipple alternately soft and hard. He writhes again, and I can't help it, I pull his hips down into mine, holding him there, needing the presence and the pressure.

He scrapes his uneven nails down my torso. Again. I don't let go of him. He drags them over me, from shoulders to hip bones, and this time, causing enough pain for me to look down. Tiny lines of blood are starting to form from torn, scratched skin. I drop my hands to my sides, and he looks at me and grins imposingly. He pulls away, long enough to unbuckle my belt and unzip my fly. He yanks at the top of my jeans and boxers and I lift my hips so he can get them down. He pushes them using one foot between my legs low down enough for me to kick them off and then he's on me again, heedlessly grating his denim-covered cock against my vulnerable one: the strange pull of his movements breaching the line between "yes" and pain. I rut against him, needy, increasing the pressure and the pain.

He shoves my hips back against the mattress—leaving me momentarily and humiliatingly thrusting into the air—then crawls down my legs until he's crouched over me. His eyes catch mine and he's making sure I'm watching. A small, desperate noise sounds at the back of my throat. Rylan grins, licks a line up the underside of my dick and swallows it down. I try to thrust upwards but he swats at my hip and I know I'm to just let this happen. He oh-so-slowly withdraws my cock from his throat, his lips releasing my cockhead with a smug popping sound. He then takes his time lapping at my cockhead, running his tongue stud along my frenulum before swallowing me down again.

He's going way too long and slow and deep for this stage in the proceedings. His fingers tease and coax at my sac and I swear, the combination of so much shit happening and so long without sex and whatever the fuck he's playing at almost makes me grip the hotel bed cover with desperation.

Of course he knows what he's doing to me, how close he's getting me, but knowing he's not giving me what I need to go over. The look in his eyes as he relinquishes my dick from his mouth tells me he's not done with me. He sits back on my shins, jerking me lazily with his hand, too loose and too slow to do anything but frustrate the hell out of me.

"Hand," he says, and the whole speaking thing takes me so off-guard that I don't immediately get what he wants. He slaps my flank sharply, simultaneously making me jump and spiking my arousal and then he just grabs at my hand and closes it over his—the one working my dick. I squeeze his fist, trying to make him jack me harder, but he resists. "Stay," he murmurs, and slides his hand out from under mine, then squeezes my hand to tighten around my dick. He watches me for a moment, eyes glinting in the fluorescent light streaming through the cheap curtains, then climbs off me, and leans against the dresser facing the bed.

I panic, hand flying off my dick, incredibly aware of how clothed he is and naked I am. I go to pull the covers over me, or something stupid, but Rylan's voice cuts me off.

"I didn't say stop." His voice is teasing and dangerous and makes my dick jump with want.

I sit up, nervous somehow, and lean tentatively against the headboard. My cock is throbbing with need, either oblivious or hypersensitive to my humiliation, and Rylan's just there, watching me, waiting. But I *can't*. When it's him touching me, I can forget; I can get lost in the physical-ness of everything, but...this. For fuck's sakes, why is he just *watching* me?

He walks back over, standing beside the bed.

"Let me show you," he reproaches me and then reaches out. My whole body blushes intensely. I feel embarrassed, dirty, stupid. He wrenches my thighs wide open and wraps one of my hands around my dick, the other he forces upwards to grip the top of the headboard. He tweaks my nipples with a calculated air of forbearance, like he's humouring me somehow. It makes my skin burn with shame and my guts squirm with arousal. "Good. Now, go." And he leaves, giving me a moment to collect myself, before reaching the dresser and turning back to face me.

I take a steadying breath. And slowly, move my hand up the length of my cock.

"Is that how you like it?" he...either teases or jeers, I can't quite tell which. "Slow and stupid?"

I grit my teeth and shake my head.

"Then show me," he demands.

I tighten my grip and close my eyes and let my head fall back against the wood panel behind me. This is quasi-foreign territory: I've never been super comfortable with masturbation—feels wrong, or like cheating or something. But knowing this is for him makes me want this: my body wants this, my cock wants this, so I find myself getting lost in it, finding my standard grip, and rhythm: upwards with quick, short, hard jerks. And I'm mounting, definitely building and it feels so fucking good, knowing he is there, watching me, knowing that I'm being good for him, knowing that he can twist my shame and want in on each other—

"Eyes on me," Rylan orders.

My eyelids fly open to look at him, and when I see him, I realize that he's jerking himself off to the sight of me and I realize that even if he's only going slowly, it still means that I....arouse him. That I turn him on like he turns me on, and even if I always knew that, I just somehow didn't *know* that and....Holy shit—that sudden knowledge makes a cry rise in my throat and my hand tighten and my hips thrust and I come, hard and sudden and loud.

He smiles while I pant, come splattered over my hand and abdomen. He gives me maybe a minute to recuperate. And then, "Stand up."

I follow his instructions almost without thinking, wiping the come off on the bedspread before balancing on shaky legs, dick slowly deflating between my thighs.

"Come here," he directs. I walk unsteadily over to him until I'm standing before him. He runs a finger down one of the scratch marks he's made on my chest. He leans in and kisses me. And it's long and slow, and his fist grips one of my wrists making me feel somehow in his possession. "You're so goddamn sexy, Niles," he whispers. I don't know how to reply. He never does this. Never says anything, except his teasing JCrew comments, about the way I look. So I don't really know how to react. He doesn't seem to mind, just kisses me for a bit longer, taking his time, running his tongue over my bottom lip before withdrawing.

"Put your hands behind your head," he directs me, his voice quiet.

I do so, slightly apprehensive. He grabs me by the wrists and walks me over to the table. He pulls one of the chairs out of the way, and bends me over, kicking my feet wide, spreading me. He turns my head so all I can see is the wall a foot or so away, or, if I look up, the corner of the hotel writing paper. Suddenly his hands are gone and I want to look around the room, to know what he's doing, but I also know I shouldn't.

"I'm gonna fuck you, soon, Nigh. Would you like that?"

I thought I was coming down, but the dark timbre of his voice makes it clear that that's not happening. Instead my cock twitches with interest and I find myself nodding minutely, cheek sticking slightly to the table top. I hear the sound of a zipper being pulled, some rustling of clothing. He pulls the chair over closer.

"Knee up on that. Brace yourself." Instinctively I do as I'm told, shoving my ass out towards him, shamelessly.

I feel something smooth and warm and big brush against the bottom of my ass crack. I know it's his cock head and it feels so good nestled up against my balls. He drags it along my crack, painstakingly slowly. He stops when he gets to my asshole and for one terror-stricken moment I'm afraid he's going to try and shove it in. I gasp and try to turn towards him, but he just holds my head against the table and chuckles.

"Relax, sugar. I'm gonna take good care of you."

I hear the pop of a lube cap and then his fingertip is there, teasing the outside of my asshole. He flickers it back and forth but doesn't go in, not until I hitch my hips backwards, desperate for more.

"Oh, I see," he chides. "You want me *in*side."

I might growl. Just a little bit.

His finger pulses forward and I bear down a bit, opening for him. I still remember when being penetrated felt weird, unnatural. Originally it had been the dirty realization, the, "Oh my God. I'm being fucked right now," that would get me off, but now it's the fucking itself. He eases his finger in, coating me with lube. I do still love the mental aspect of it— the knowing that he's opening me to take his cock, to bring him pleasure. He coaxes his finger in and out of me until I'm ready for another. I live for the burning-stretching feeling that only lasts a few moments as he increases the diameter.

"Hungry little hole, aren't you?" he murmurs and I fucking do not understand why we've never included dirty talk (or any talk) in our sex before, because it is the actual best thing.

Three fingers and I'm silently begging for his cock. He's careful, as he always is, not to overdo the prep—it's like he knows without me ever telling him that I want the tight discomfort that comes when I'm just shy of ready. Soon, and yet somehow not soon enough, his cock head touches my hole. I try to cant back onto it, but he slaps my ass—hard and makes a "tch"ing noise.

"I decide when you get my cock, not you," he scolds.

God. His stupid perfect mouth and his stupid perfect words. My cock searches the air desperately for something to rub up against but is disappointed. And, in that moment, Rylan enters me fully. I grunt with the force of him—it was too hard and too fast and too much to feel good and for those very reasons it *does* feel good. His cock feels bigger than I know it actually is, but maybe this time even more so, maybe because I haven't had him for so long. With one hand he grips my wrists which are still clasped behind my head, aching with their obedient stillness, and with the other his fingers bite into my hip. And then, finally, blessedly, he fucks me.

He pulls his cock almost all the way out of me before slamming back in. He likes it slow and long on the way out, and quick on the way in, at least to begin with. The back of my mind mumbles something about condoms but I shut it down, too far gone to give a shit because all I know is that when he's out I feel too empty and when he's in I feel too full and I guess that makes sense, because with Rylan I never have a sense of equilibrium.

He bites into my shoulder blade, and then shifts his hand to clutch aggressively at my ass, and here I am, splayed and open, bent over a table, being fucked, forcefully and I want it so much I can't stand it. I crave it and him inside me, and it's a craving that can't be sated even with him pounding my ass into a hotel table, it just makes me want him more: deeper, fiercer. I want him to fuck me within an inch of my life, want him to come, to soak me with his cum, want to know that I did that, I made him come. I tighten slightly around him and he groans, and it's that groan that I love the most, the knowledge that I have that ability, that I get to hear that, and…maybe no one else does.

"Fuck, Niles," he whispers desperately into my ear, and my dick twinges wantonly in response. He's quickening the pace, and fumbling for my cock, and his thrusts are becoming more shallow and his finger nails bite into me again, and he thrusts so so so hard, one, two, three, four and I feel him coming inside me, one-two-three-four and he holds there, in me, where he strokes me to completion, knowing I'm full of him. He collapses on me and we breathe together for a long moment before he pulls out and wipes himself off and pushes me against the wall, his cum seeping out of me, and kisses me, lips drawing me into him, then forcing me backwards. And I'm naked and he's clothed and he's kissing me still until finally he whispers that I should go shower, and me? I obey.

- 10 -

My whole body is zinging. I can't concentrate on anything for long. In the shower, the water washing down the drain is light pink at first from the scratches on my chest and stomach. I turn the heat way, way up and just let everything hurt. I dry off and pull on some underwear but I don't get dressed. I'd just get little sticks of blood on a shirt right now anyway.

When I come back into the room, Rylan is sitting on the far bed, something in his hand. He looks up. I walk over to him, too simultaneously relaxed and energized to feel self-conscious. I sit next to him. He holds out a tube of antibacterial goop.

"Here. For your battle wounds," he explains, fingering one of the tiny lines of blood droplets forming on my abs.

"You do it," I say, flopping backwards on the bed. "You made them, you fix them." It's so amazingly liberating to talk like this, to acknowledge what happened just actually happened—that mentioning it is somehow allowed.

He applies the greasy gel studiously to each one of the numerous scratches individually. It doesn't sting or anything, but I'm guessing they will start to by tomorrow.

"Sit up and I'll do your back," Ry offers.

"They're on my back?" I didn't know, I have no recollection of...but I was pretty distracted. I sit up, granting him access. I can barely feel his fingertips as he carefully smoothes the cream into my skin. Finally, his fingers pause. He drops his forehead onto my shoulder. I'm almost positive he's about to speak, so I stay quiet. I hear him lick his lips and sigh very softly.

"Niles," he says, and I can feel it in my stomach, this is going to be something big, something we've never said before. "Look. I...I would never cheat on you."

I don't have a ready response for that, so he plows right on. "Just in case, you know, that's what the condom thing was about. I know I reacted shittily but. I don't know. It hurt that you thought that I would cheat. I would never cheat."

The words are there and I know I shouldn't say them but for some reason I can't stop myself because I'm angry. Because he's got all the cards, he's always had all the cards and I'm always guessing. "You can't cheat. That would imply that we were in an actual relationship."

There's a pause or beat or something. Like in a script. Like... *beat*.

"What do you...mean by that?" he asks carefully. Trying so hard not to accuse that it comes out suspicious anyway.

What does he mean what do I mean? I don't know. It would mean that we had something that we don't. So far as I can tell. At least nothing he's admitted to and that's fucking shitty of him. But I've already used up my courage and I'm already unravelling and terrified that I've gone and done a thing that will make him leave and I don't want that, I just don't—and so I chicken out.

"What do you think I mean?"

"Um. That you don't think we're in a relationship?" His voice is firm. Or scared. Or an obscure mixture of both.

"Well. We're not. Not really."

He lifts his forehead off my shoulder and my body mourns the loss and a detached sort of nausea settles in.

"Oh."

He stands, wipes his hands on his jeans and then slides them into his pockets. He doesn't look at me. His eyes are on the window. This isn't what I was expecting. I don't know what I was expecting. Probably for this conversation to never happen. Or for him to be the one telling me that we weren't actually together and not the other way around. But I went and said it, the truth, and he's just standing there, spine slumping and—I'm almost positive—defeated.

And even though I don't know how I wanted this to go, or if I wanted it to go at all, I *do* know that I don't want it to go like this.

"What?" The word is a whisper because I don't know what else to say.

He doesn't answer.

"Ry, what?" There is a note of pleading in my voice that I hate but can't shake.

He still just stares out the seagull-shit-stained window.

"So, we're not actually together."

A definite edge of coldness. I'm in uncharted waters here. Possibly drowning. So instead of answering I shrug.

"So the last three years have been...what?" he pushes.

Again I haven't got any sort of answer.

"Like...a joke? A game? Some sort of experiment?"

Fuck! I don't know! He's the one who's been in charge here. I'm just...along for the ride. I mean. This is what I wanted, right? Wanted him to say we were really together, that my fears were pathetically unwarranted. That I'm an idiot and he loves me and I really have nothing to worry about. But for some stupid reason I can't say that. I can't tell him what I want to hear, even though now because I'm petrified and my tongue is useless in my mouth and I just *can't*.

"I don't know," I murmur.

"You don't know." I watch his shoulders tense in silhouette.

"Ry..." I offer, helplessly.

"What?" he snarls and turns on me, finally, his face screwed up with anger and making me wish he'd stayed looking at the window because I've never seen him like this, except maybe for the condom thing and I hate him like this. He's not *him* like this.

"I..." Can't speak. I can't.

"What the hell are you doing with me, then?" He's livid now, with a fearsome quality to his eyes that I've never seen, even when he's holding me down.

"I..."

"You," he echoes nastily.

Fuck. He's going to walk out. He's going to turn and leave before I ever can spit out what I'm trying to say.

"I don't..." I try again.

"How many people are you sleeping with?" he hisses, leaning into me. "All this time, I thought you belonged to me, with me, but maybe you've got a dozen others hooked in to your fucking little innocent, untouchable, unreachable scheme. Have them all fucked up and in love with you, just like me. You think it's a good game, hey? Fucking with people?"

"No! I..."

I want to explain. I need to tell him. But I don't know what I need to tell him, I can't remember what's the truth. If I'm the one that loves him or he's the one that loves me and who's been keeping what a secret all this time. I can't keep track of all the shit we don't tell each other.

"How many!" he demands. He jerks his hand as if to grab my arm but stops himself, arm suspended in mid-air.

"You!" I gasp out. "Just you. Fuck, just you."

He turns away again. "Put on some fucking clothes," he orders. "I can't concentrate with you sitting there like that."

I remain frozen, dumbfounded for a minute, waiting for him to recant that, he can't mean it. He waits, then turns and watches me as I slide on some jeans and one of his T-shirts, one that obnoxiously hangs off him like some '90s relic, but fits me. Shit.

"OK," I say, quietly. I don't even know.

"OK," he echoes, voice hollowed.

Fuck. I need to fix this. I never fix anything. I'm an adamant disciple of avoiding an issue until it goes away, but I know I can't do this this time. It's too goddamn important. I *need* to fix this. I walk to him and stand uselessly in front of him like some shy, dopey sixth grader who doesn't know what to do with his hands on a first date.

"I...didn't mean it like that."

"Oh, really." His voice is cold, sarcastic, detached. "Because there are so many ways 'we're not in an actual relationship' can be taken."

"I know. I know. I'm sorry, I'm stupid, it's stupid. I'm sorry." I can't tell if I'm talking or sobbing, my breath is so shallow and desperate.

"What's stupid?" he answers, and I think there's a tinge of generosity, or compassion there—or at least something more than anger.

"Me. I'm an idiot. A huge idiot. Colossal, even."

He waits.

"It's just...Fuck, Ry. We don't...talk. About it. So I didn't know, because...you never say..."

Shock clouds Rylan's expression. "*We* don't talk about it? WE? You've got to be kidding me, Niles. *You* don't talk about anything! You don't initiate ANYTHING. You leave me hanging here in limbo. Permanently wondering if you're going to answer the next time I call, if you even want me to call, if...if fucking EVERYTHING. I don't talk because you so obviously can't handle it. And I am trying to be patient, just give you some fucking time. I mean, coming out and everything is a big thing, and I know that, and you've got family you didn't want to disappoint, but they don't care. And we've got straight friends, but they don't give a shit, and so I've just been waiting and waiting and fucking waiting for you to tell me the capacity in which I exist to you, and you never, ever do. And this has been going on for three fucking years! I've been waiting for three years for you to just be able to say it, and you haven't! All you can tell me is that you didn't know we were even a thing? What the fuck am I supposed to do with that? Are you seriously just trying to—to wreck me?"

"I'm sorry," I whisper. It's all I can come up with.

"Don't," he says, "Please don't. Don't be sorry. Don't just sit there and say useless things. Tell me what is going on or how it got to this, or fucking anything, really, but please don't just not talk. I can't stand another minute of not talking."

And...it's actually terrifying? Because I want so, so much to just lie down and close my eyes, stop thinking, stop moving, even, because somehow I know if I did, no matter how much he'd want to get up and leave, eventually he'd lie down too and hold me up against him and we'd never have to say a word about this again. But I can't do that. He...fucking...bought my little sister a book about sharks, and gives an actual shit about my family, and he takes me to the symphony and he can read me, in sex and life and sleep, and he knows what to do with me even when I don't know what to do with myself. So I say it. It's thick and bulky and unused, but it's true.

"I love you."

His eyes bore into mine—I wanted it to be enough but he's still waiting.

"I seriously do," I insist. "I love you so much that mostly all I can think about is what will happen when I lose you."

"You're not going to lose me," he says incredulously. "Where the fuck would I go?"

"I don't know! I just know that…I don't know. Fuck. Like…the girl. Woman. The bride, you know, at the club?"

"Tell me you're joking."

"What? Why?"

"The bride, Niles? Seriously?"

"Yes, the bride, seriously! She was all over you and you were all over her and it was like you were putting on a show about how much you didn't need me."

"Jesus Christ, Nigh. You have it, like, absolutely ass-backwards. Can I tell you what was going on there? Which I would have told you if you'd asked. Or I would have told you if I thought for even a second that it would have crossed your mind that I want anyone other than you?"

I don't give him an answer and he doesn't wait for one.

"Look. She comes up to me and is all, 'So…I know this is totally un-PC of me, but my girlfriends dragged me here and said I needed to find a man on my so-called last night of freedom, and I know it's stupid, but I don't want to disappoint them, because they put all this energy into this thing and I'm actually a total people-pleaser, but I'm really not that interested in like, you know, hooking up with anyone, so…Are you gay? And I'm not asking that because you are flamboyant or anything, not that there's anything wrong with being flamboyant, it's just I saw you kissing a dude, so I'm hoping you won't hate me for asking to participate in a little charade?' And I said something like, 'Happy to help a lady out!' And then we danced and hung out long enough to satisfy her friends. Do you see where I'm going with this, Niles? She was dancing with me because I am gay and she didn't want to feel like she was cheating."

"Oh."

"Yeah. Oh, and by the way, Nigh, I'm gay. Really fucking gay. I am into men. Not women. Men. And not just any men, but a specific one in particular, namely, in case you haven't noticed, *you*. Do you get me?"

I nod and feel like a general idiot-freak.

"Do you hate me for being such a douche?" I mumble.

"I believe the term is douchius," he corrects, smiling a little. "And no. Never."

He puts his arms around me, finally, letting me hide my stupid face in his bony shoulder.

"You OK?" he asks.

"Yeah," I breathe. "It's just...fuck. There's so much stuff we've never talked about, so much stuff we've avoided..."

"Like what?"

I lift my head and step back enough to see his face. Rylan's arms slide down mine 'til we're carefully holding each other's forearms. "I don't know...anything my apparently neurotic brain deemed taboo?"

He looks at me curiously. "Like...?"

"I dunno! Like sex. Or us. Or how we started, or when we started, or what we do, or what we're doing."

"Do you want to? I mean, I'm happy to, but talking doesn't seem to be your absolute favourite thing."

"Well. Yeah. I guess I think I do. Like...I don't even know how you decided to...make a move that first morning."

Rylan snorts. "I have no idea how I decided either. I was terrified I would permanently screw things up between us. Thought you would shove me off, or knee me in the balls, and I'd be lucky if you passed it off as us being drunk."

"I thought about it," I offer, and then clarify, "The drunk thing. Not the other stuff."

"Ha. Thanks." He pauses. "I'm pretty glad you didn't."

I shrug. "One of the smarter things I've done in regards to you, apparently."

"Yup. See? You're not a complete fuck up." He shakes my arms gently to show he's joking.

"Fuck you!" I counter, with next to no venom.

He laughs and for a second we're quiet, until suddenly he's pushed me backwards and is straddling me on the bed, arms around my neck, face so close me mine we're almost touching.

"I love you," he says. "An unsurpassable amount."

I blush stupidly and slide my hands over his ass and he kisses my face.

"I would do anything for you," he continues, and there's a weightiness to his voice that wasn't there a second ago.

"I know..."

He shakes his head. "No, Niles, I don't think you do. I don't think you could. Because I mean *anything*. You've got your family. I know that. But me...you're what I've got. Like it sounds a bit fucked up, but you're it. So...you get the whole undiluted devotion. The anything." His tone lightens. "So if you want me to use a condom, I most certainly will..."

"Fuck no. No condom. Worst idea I ever had."

His arms tighten around my neck and he throws his head back and laughs. I kiss his throat and squeeze his ass and run my hands over his thighs and he waits for me, lets me be the one to close the distance, to slip his shirt over his upstretched arms, to press my lips against his chest and flip him.

He lies beneath me, calm and curious. I undress us both and we're naked together for the first time tonight. He runs his palms along my forearms and I feel bigger, stronger, more powerful than him, and I have a weird surge of protectiveness that I've never really experienced. Rylan smiles like maybe he knows what I'm thinking and maybe he doesn't but it's actually OK either way.

I kiss his neck and jaw and chest and it seems beyond bizarre that I haven't really done this before: been this

95

complicit, this participatory. He rolls his hips where they lie beneath mine. Neither one of us is very hard, yet. I kiss his face once more before standing and hunting out the lube, then wet my palm with it and toss it on the bedspread. I take both our cocks together, spreading the fluid over them both and it just feels...really fucking nice. Rylan hooks his heels around my thighs and sighs happily.

"God, you feel good," he says, and it's not dirty talk, it is just Rylan-brand genuinity.

And he feels good, too. I rut against him, sliding my fist, now joined by his, up and down both our stalks. The soft-hard slide of his cock against mine is nothing short of fan-fucking-tastic.

"Fuck. Ry," I mutter into his neck, just because I can, because talking is a thing we do now. He groans happily and hikes his legs higher on mine. I remove my hand, reluctantly, from our cocks and reach for the lube. "I want to fuck you," I find myself saying. "Can I?"

"God, yes," he replies, unravelling his legs from my body and tucking them up to his chest.

I've never seen him like this: pliable and mild. It's not what I'm used to, or even what I especially like, but for now—it's good or right or something. I stroke his balls and jack his cock for a moment before gently introducing my finger, palm up. He exhales carefully and I know he's adjusting. I never fuck him. He fucks himself on me, sure, but this? It's different and I don't want to fuck it up.

"Don't let me hurt you," I whisper.

He laughs. "I'm not exactly some shrinking flower or wilting violet or whatever."

"I know. I just..." I mumble, stupidly.

"Don't worry," he says. "Feels good. Fuck me with it for a bit."

I am, as usual, happy and relieved to take direction and pulse my finger in and out of him, watching his asshole spread tidily around my finger like it was meant just for me. The idea makes my erection twinge in anticipation.

"It's good. Another," Rylan instructs. I am happy to oblige and start fucking two fingers in and out of him, scissoring them gently. As Rylan opens for me, I curl my fingers, striking his prostate and listening to him squeal with pleasure. The heady power of it is addictive and I stroke it over and over, watching him writhe and curse beneath me. I add another finger, but within a few moments he's crying out.

"Jesus, fuck, Nigh. If you don't fuck me right now, I swear to fucking God I'm going to come and you will so regret it!"

I really don't need much more encouragement than that. I grip his skinny hips with my hands and tilt his pelvis upwards. He hooks a heel over my shoulder, the other knee still against his chest so that it's not too intense too soon. I grip my dick and guide it into him and he hisses slightly at the snug fit.

"Fuck. Fuck. Fuck," I find myself sputtering. "Fuck, Ry, fuck you feel so fucking good."

He grins. "Good. Give me a moment and then you can fuck me."

I'm not actually sure I can't wait a moment without coming, but I'm damn sure going to try.

"OK," he says. "It's good, babe. Fuck me."

I thrust slowly back and forth inside of him and he gasps and grips my neck and kisses me. I kiss him back, and hold his ass tight, pressing his body into mine, so that even when I fuck back there's no loss of contact between us.

And it is like this that I take him, feeling his body roll with mine. Mouth to neck, chest to back, palm to hip and, brilliantly, words to skin.

- Part Two -

- 11 -

"What's wrong with your leg?"

Rylan finishes pulling on his jeans and eyes me appraisingly. "You're kidd—you're serious." He raises an eyebrow at me.

"What?"

He shakes his head at me, bewildered, before his face cracks into a grin. "Ain't nothing wrong with my leg, darlin'," he drawls, fake accent and everything. He does this sometimes, says it appeals to my Albertan heritage. Ha ha, funny, right? Except not.

"You're limping," I insist, because I'm not being derailed that easily. So I'm a little paranoid about health stuff right now, no surprises there.

"I am," he agrees, hilarity dancing in his eyes. Too bad I'm not in on the joke. "But it's nothing to do with my legs."

I just look at him. Sometimes he makes no sense whatsoever.

He shakes his head, obviously amused. "Oooohhh, Nigh Uncanny. For all I've put you through, you've remained incredibly sweet and innocent."

He stretches, shirtless, scratches his belly and heads towards the bathroom, leaning in as he passes me and whispering, "I'm limping because you fucked me so goddamn good last night." He pats me happily on the cheek, and, smiling like a Joe Boxer trademark, strolls right on by.

Well. Obviously. Right. Or it should be, but of course it wasn't at all. It didn't even cross my mind—I mean, to still feel it in the morning? I didn't go very hard...except that, well, I don't usually, you know, go at all, unless I'm really drunk or unless he...does it himself. And then I guess he kinda...monitors progress. Shit.

I follow after him, determined, now that we're talking, to talk about this. He's shaving, smiles at me in the mirror when I enter.

"What's up?" he asks casually.

"I didn't mean to hurt you," I spit up.

He eyes me curiously. "You didn't..."

"You're limping..."

"Yeah, but that's just a matter of disuse. I never said I didn't like it..."

What. Does he...This one is a curve ball. I mean. I'd always just assumed that he liked to control and I liked to be controlled, and that was that. I mean, I like that, a lot. I've always liked that. I like routine.

"Oh..." I respond.

Rylan looks at me like he can't quite read me and like maybe he finds that intriguing somehow. He rinses his razor and grazes over the spot in front of his ear.

"What?" he prods.

"Nothing," I say, too quickly.

"Yeah right, Nigh, what?" He isn't intense about it, just interested. I don't know what he finds so interesting, other than my obvious inability to communicate even simple sentences.

"I don't know. Just...do you like that? I mean, are you...not liking our...I mean are you unhappy..." I peter out uselessly.

He washes the remnants of shaving cream off his face. "Are you asking if I'm unsatisfied with our sex life?"

Yes. That is what I mean. Now why wasn't I able to just put it out there? I nod, just barely, because what if I don't want to know?

"Not even sort of. I am—incredibly, unbelievably satisfied. Are you unhappy with it?"

"No. Jesus. God. No," I say immediately, grateful that my voice sounds certain, responsive, and not defensive.

"I just meant it was...nice," he settles on finally. "To switch things up. But....I prefer things the way they usually are."

"Me too." I still have a hard time believing I'm actually talking about this, out loud, to someone who isn't Shona.

"OK, good." He gives me a little grin, and splashes water over his face, then wipes his chin off with a hand towel. "So we both like things the way we do things—why are you looking at me like something really awful is going to happen?"

With that, I feel all this stress or tension or uncertainty or *something* I didn't even know I was carrying just drop out of my shoulders and neck and back. Because he's right. I'm acting all neurotic and estranged and that is ridiculous. I let myself relax finally, shaking my head and smiling.

"I have no idea."

"You're such a nut, Captain," he says affectionately, slipping his hand up to my neck and then kissing me.

And I guess now it's like this. Now he will stay after we fuck and not only will he stay, but he'll kiss me. His tongue prods at my lips to open and they do so quite willingly. So we're kissing now. But it's nice to know that when we stop, I'll be able to say anything I want.

* * *

So it turns out something really awful was about to happen. The week after we get home, Mom calls to say that Kya's operation is scheduled the day after her friend Cole's funeral. So Dad, Matilda, and Rylan and I all go back to Vancouver for the week, and at Kya's request, to attend the service. It's without doubt the most depressing thing I've ever been to. Picture a good two hundred people, all connected to this poor kid in some way, standing there in teary-eyed, miserable shock. There's flowers and soccer cleats and his famous flipbooks and those frickin' origami paper cranes his classmates made him (fucking lot of good that did), which makes me feel bad for the kids. I mean, their hope is totally quashed. You could pick them out, the kids in his class, looking lost between their parents, miserable in formal clothing.

Kya refuses to stay home and rest the day like she's supposed to. Instead she stands, dry-eyed, like a miniature military wife who accepted the whole fucking deal and now has to live with it. But she gets it, knew this was coming.

It doesn't make any sense though, I keep telling myself. She's seven. She's always been obnoxious, but never dramatic or intense and then suddenly, it's just...wham. Suddenly she's forty or sixty or...it's not even age. I mean, she's seven. But she looks like she's done or seen so much. I can't explain. She is oblivious to Matilda holding her hand, or Mom dabbing her eyes every couple of minutes through the long, gut-wrenching service. They show video clips and pictures and family friends tell stories and even though I never even met the kid, he really meant something to Kya and that shreds me up a bit. The videos make it clear that Cole was a cheeky, pretentious little bugger. Sharp and cynical and...a bit like Rylan, and that freaks me out.

I don't cry. I mean, I feel like crying, but I don't because, well, I don't tend to cry, but also because I feel like it's not my grief, that I don't have the right to cry. That anything I'm feeling, like this...jackhammer of sadness on my sternum, must be amplified a thousand times over for his family. So I can't miss him, I can just sit there and feel really, really sorry for his family, and for Kya.

Rylan's a bit of a mess, too. While my father drives us all back to the hotel in the minivan, Ry just sits there, shivering and scratching his elbow and staring at nothing, ignoring the fact that he's crying and sniffing all over the place. And there's nothing anyone can say. You can't say, "Well, that was a nice service," or, "Well, he lived a good life," like you can after old people's funerals. Nope. This whole thing is just...really shitty.

In the car I keep my hand on Rylan's thigh, and he grabs at it almost fretfully every once in a while, squeezing. Kya gets up on her knees on the seat in front of us and turns around.

"Kya, sit back down," my mom says tiredly.

"Don't worry," Kya says, ignoring our mother and peering through the space between the seat and the headrest, focusing on Rylan. "*I'm* not going to die."

"You could if you don't get your bum back on that seat," my mother insists.

Rylan offers her a watery smile.

"I'm only getting an eye cut out. And did you know that afterwards, they are gonna put in like a boob implant, except for instead of for my boobie it's going to be for my eye."

That sets Mom off crying again, and Rylan starts laughing and Matilda wraps her arm around Kya's shoulder.

It might seem like a bit of an adventure to Kya, but the rest of us are pretty shaken up by the whole thing. I keep thinking of all the things she'll have trouble with, like what if she wants to take up, like, archery or something? I just want her to be able to do anything and what if she can't?

Rylan and I wait in the hotel room with my parents until Kya falls asleep, and then we head off to our own room. There, we climb into bed and curl in on each other, wordlessly knowing that we have escaped tragedy.

* * *

105

"OK, before you say anything, hear me out," Rylan is saying. We're back at home on the island, and in a few days, Kya will have recovered enough from her surgery to come home, permanently.

"Because phrasing something like that doesn't make me at all uneasy..." I respond. Rylan's sitting cross-legged and sideways on the couch in my apartment, leaning in towards me earnestly.

"Well, you're going to think I'm being an insensitive dickwad, but then you'll think about it, and you'll know I'm right."

"Not helping," I tell him.

"I know. OK, here it is: I think that when Kya gets home, we should have a pirate party."

At first, I don't get it. "A pirate party?" I echo.

"Yeah, you know, with like peg-legs and, I don't know, kegs of orange pop, and, um, eye patches."

And *then* I get it. "Eye patches?"

"Yeah..." He looks at me helplessly.

"Um. Nope, pretty sure that is a horrible idea and that you are, in fact, an insensitive dickwad."

"No!" Rylan shifts restlessly onto his knees and braces an enthusiastic hand on my shoulder. "I mean, with a normal kid, it would be totally cruel, but, Nigh, this is *Kya*. She'll love it, you know she will..."

It's wrong, but he's right. She will love it.

"A pirate party," I repeat again.

Rylan slides closer and swings a knee over so he's straddling me. He rubs his hands up my chest teasingly. "I'll get a piñata shaped like a treasure chest..." he tempts.

"Jesus. I'll get the piñata. You convince my family that this is somehow sane," I resolve.

"You're on." He grins, and takes my lower lip teasingly between his teeth before kissing me fully.

* * *

Rylan goes all out. He borrows two huge fish tanks from his work, and fixes them with electric blue light bulbs. He hangs cardboard lanterns from the ceiling and throws ratty blankets over all the couches in my parents' living room. He gets in touch with Kya's teacher and arranges for invitations to be sent home with all the kids in her class. I'm worried none of them will show just because of the tactlessness of it all, but Rylan sends a black eye patch along with every single invitation anyway. He gets himself a Seinfeld-esque puffy shirt, and cuts it open down the front, manages to locate some black and white striped clam-digger pants, and a bright red sash to use as a belt. He gets both of us swords.

"Annnnnd," he says, pulling the last of the items out of his thrift store bags, with a flourish. "For you, Captain!" He wields a brown tricorne, complete with an ostentatious ostrich feather. He knows I'm not really into dressing up, but he also knows I can't turn down a hat. Next, he pulls out a T-shirt with a Jolly Roger on it. "That should fit," he says, grinning. I change in the bathroom at my folks' house. The kids will be arriving soon, once school gets out.

Matilda skips her last block, and, having caught some of Rylan's enthusiasm, is dressed up in a peasant blouse and headscarf. Her friend Courtney stands awkwardly nearby, eye patch resting on top of her forehead.

"Til, you look fantastic!" Rylan grins, swooping her up in a hug before making easy small talk with Courtney, who seems to relax under the attention.

The doorbell rings and kids in various pirate get-ups begin to appear. I am relieved to realize that most parents decided a kid with cancer takes priority over political correctness. Rylan hands out orange crush and plastic swords, and, as battles and cardboard prisons and the sounds of what I think are supposed to be cannonballs begin to take over the room, Kya comes home.

Her eye patch is bright orange and has sequins. She looks around rather stunned for a minute, and then lets out a mighty war whoop and jumps right on in. My dad leads my mom into the kitchen, both of them looking rather bewildered.

Shona arrives a bit later, and she and I take over first aid and fish tank patrol, making sure no orange pop ends up in the fish tanks. Rylan is too busy leaping around shouting, "Arr! Matey!"—much to the delight of the second-graders—to pay attention to his beloved fish friends. After cake and sparklers and one episode involving orange vomit, Rylan eventually sends the kids on their way, carrying paper bags of gold-wrapped coins, candy cigars and plastic kazoos. Kya is passed out in a sugar coma on the couch, and my parents and I are puttering around clearing up streamers and paper cups.

Rylan flops on the couch, obviously pleased with himself, and Kya wakes up enough to crawl on top of him, announcing that this was the best non-birthday birthday party ever. Kya insists on fish-sticks for dinner, followed by a viewing of the entire *Pirates of the Caribbean* series. I'm dead to the world by halfway through the second one, but a few hours later, Rylan wakes me up to drag me to bed, and Kya is now sitting, wired, in front of the TV.

"I love those movies!" she sighs happily.

"Really?" I ask. "Because you've only watched them about six million times, so how can you be sure?"

"NILES!" She pounces on me and I sling her over my shoulder. We all brush our teeth for, like, eight minutes solid, until there are no remnants of orange dye to be seen anywhere. Rylan kisses me on the ear, exhausted, his arm draped over my chest. He then pads away to my old room. I walk with Kya to her room, taking responsibility for the tucking-in ritual.

"I'm never getting a glass eye," Kya tells me as she squirms into her covers.

"Oh yeah? Why's that?"

"No one else gets to wear an eye patch in class. They'd get told to take it off."

Can't argue with logic.

I cuddle back into Kya's pillows, taking up too much room in her small bed, but she doesn't seem to mind, just drops her head on my shoulder and whispers, "He made me promise."

I peer down at her, thinking she's sleep-talking gibberish, or something, but she's not. She's staring at me intently.

"Who made you promise what, Ky?"

"Cole. He made me promise. I just don't want you to think that I don't miss him. Because I do, so so so so so so so much."

"I know you do, Kya-bear, I never thought you didn't." I tuck a runaway piece of hair behind her ear.

"But he made me promise that I wouldn't be sad. He said that if I was just sad then I'd miss everything and then I'd hate him for missing everything, and he didn't want me to hate him, ever. I'm trying so so so so so so so hard to be fun and happy, so that he knows. I need him to know that I would never ever hate him. So I can't be sad. But," she bites her lip fiercely, "even when I don't want to, sometimes I can't help it. He would've thought today was the serious best."

A couple of tears sneak out even though she's fighting it, and she bats at them angrily. I run my hand over the back of her head and I tell her that he knows, that I'm certain of it, and when she asks why, I tell her that when you love somebody that much, they will always just know. But, just in case, once Kya's asleep, I make the few steps into my old room, and slip into my old bed and I let Rylan know, just in case he doesn't, that I love him that much.

- 12 -

"So things are good, then?" Shona's asking, frowning at her just-waxed eyebrows in the mirror in an effort to glare the redness away, "With you and the boy?"

"Yes," I smile. "Things are good. Great, even."

"Communication's a beautiful thing," she spouts obnoxiously, then, turning towards me, "See any stragglers?" She motions towards her eyebrows.

"None. They look lovely, well worth your nine dollars."

"You're telling me. So you and Rylan. Happy and talking and rendering me virtually obsolete?"

I shrug. "I'm sure he'll eventually do something to piss me off and you know I'll come ranting to you."

"You'd better." She watches me for a second, until I start to feel a slight blush creep up on my neck, like there's something I should've noticed but just haven't.

"What?"

"How did you do it?" she asks, finally, and her voice is muted, especially for Shona.

"How did I do what?"

"How did you manage to bring up in conversation how he pretty much drunkenly strangled you? I mean, that just seems like it could be a touchy subject."

"He didn't strangle me!" I protest immediately. "And we didn't talk about that, like, explicitly."

"Excuse me?" Shona looks personally affronted, or maybe worse; maybe just furious.

"It didn't exactly come up. We were dealing with other shit, like Kya and stuff."

"So when you say you've talked about everything, what you really mean is you're going to keep dodging the ever-growing elephant in the room and he's just going to continue doing whatever he likes to you, regardless of, you know, your health and continued survival."

"Jesus, Shona, you make it sound like I'm a fucking battered wife or something!" I'm getting frustrated now. I know she loves me, that she's just looking out for me, like she always is, but, I mean, Rylan's and my sex life is something she's always claimed not to understand, so why is she acting like she gets it all of the sudden?

"Well, maybe you're acting like one! Like, do you even hear yourself? It's always, 'He's not hurting me,' and, 'He didn't mean it like that,' and now, 'We've talked about it,' and then it turns out that you haven't. He fucking choked you, Nigh. He made you actually fearful for your actual life and he doesn't even seem bothered or remorseful enough to discuss it."

"We talked enough, OK, Shone? We covered that we're in a relationship, and have been for the last three years—"

"Nice of him to let you know," she bites.

"Well, it was stupid of me not to ask," I counter.

"I hate how he always makes you feel like you're in the wrong."

"He *never* makes me feel like that!" I can feel the unusual sensation of anger thrumming under my skin.

"Bullshit. You're Niles. You'll take whatever shit people sling at you if you think it'll make them feel better."

I stand staring at her, lower lip hovering and bobbing like an idiot. I...I just don't know how to react. Shona sighs and stands up. She walks over and puts her hands on my shoulders.

"I'm sorry, babe," she says. "I shouldn't say stupid shit like that." She nuzzles her forehead up against mine. "It's just...you are so amazing, and kind and supportive that I'm constantly terrified people will try to take advantage of you. It's stupid, I know. You're an adult. You can take care of yourself. I'm just being stupid and protective and saying things I shouldn't."

I want to cry again. I want to erase this whole conversation.

"Come on," I say, "I'll take you out for milkshakes."

* * *

"Hey, Nigh," Rylan answers the door to his apartment, looking surprised, but pleased. "Whatcha doing here?" I shuffle my feet guiltily. Even though we're supposedly doing the talking thing now, I still find myself unwilling to be the one who phones or shows up, or suggests doing something. I dunno. Even though Rylan has never made me feel like he wouldn't want to see me, I sometimes still get this weird feeling that I would be interrupting or being annoying or something.

I shrug. "Just wanted to see you," I offer, lamely.

"What's wrong?" Rylan demands. He moves out of the doorway and into the hall, allowing me to enter.

"Nothing."

"Liar." He grabs my wrists. "Come here."

He kisses me softly. Kicks the door closed behind me. I let my eyelids fall shut. This is nice.

His lips drift over to my ear. "Do you wanna talk it out, or fuck it out?"

I laugh a little, am relieved maybe. "I dunno."

"Hmmm?" He licks my earlobe. His hands toy with the bottom of my sweater. His palms conform to my hips and his breath is warm where it catches in the shell of my ear.

His fingers walk their way up my stomach, over my ribs, and then slide back down, meeting in the small of my back. He kisses my neck, my pulse point, the hollow of my throat.

"You know," he whispers, tugging at the hem of my sweater, "If I pull this off, it'll be too late for talking..."

I lift my hands above my head.

"Excellent choice," Rylan grins.

We have all afternoon. All night, if we want. I feel guilty for taking up all of Rylan's day off, but I try to shove that thought away, because he certainly doesn't seem all that upset about it. He sinks his teeth into the front of my shoulder. It hurts, but that seems to be what he's after. He slips a hand over my definitely hardening dick as if in confirmation.

"Nigh," he says, his voice dangerous and low, "undress me."

I hurry to obey and he watches me almost lazily as I unbutton his collared, mustard-coloured shirt, and tip it off his shoulders, revealing his torso. Seeing him there spurs on the realization that I honestly do know what I'm doing, because this is Rylan and I *know* him, I just do. I kiss his mouth first and then his collarbone, tentatively, awaiting signs of approval. He groans quietly, appreciatively, and I glow with pride, or pleasure, or both. I toy very lightly with his nipples, just running the pads of my thumbs over them with no intention of roughness. Rylan's like a giant house cat: pleasure or nothing. That's why I know it's a pretty big sacrifice for him to let me top. He doesn't really like it, doesn't quite think it's worth it, I guess.

I shuck off my pants and boxers and kneel before him, efficiently unbuckling his belt and pulling his boxer-briefs over his erection and down, bringing his jeans with them. He steps gracefully out of them. I wait for instruction.

"Open your mouth." His voice is quiet, calm. He holds his full cock in one hand. "Look at me."

I am obedient. I peer up at him almost shyly through my eyelashes and open my mouth, but just a bit.

He cups my face with one hand and steps closer so that his dick consumes almost my entire field of vision.

"Just a little wider, baby boy," he directs. "Show me where you want it."

I allow my jaw to relax a little wider, my lips forming a loose O. My tongue drifts forward towards my front teeth and I can hear Rylan smiling as he encourages me.

"Oh, that's very nice," he says, resting his cock head on the flat surface of my tongue. "You're so beautiful with a cock in your mouth." I can feel a little pearl of pre-cum sliding onto my tongue, but he hasn't given me permission to do anything, so I don't. It slips along the edge of his dick and collects on my lip. He chuckles darkly and withdraws, then uses his cock head to smear the bead of pre-cum over my lips. "Do you want me to feed you my cock, baby?" he asks and I swear he sounds almost loving.

I can feel the warmth of him, resting on my bottom lip, his hand cupping my face. His dark pubic hair comes in and out of focus in front of me, and I do. I do want him to—I do want that. I nod, very slightly, so as not to disturb his cock from its perch.

"Good," he croons, and his thumb rubs a gentle circle just below my cheekbone. "Keep your hands on your knees."

He slowly guides his cock into my mouth and I love the warm, sliding feeling of it over my tongue. I close my lips gently around the stalk and he sighs softly. "That's my boy," he says. His cock head bumps up against the back of my throat and my reflexes start, slightly. I repress a gag. He strokes the back of my head, leaning over me. "That's it, baby. Keep breathing. Let me in." There's another nudge against my tonsils. I tilt my head back, straightening my throat, and swallow. Rylan follows the motion with his cock, and I coax him deeper with my tongue. There's a moment's resistance, but Ry persists, pushes until his cock is seated deep in my throat. His hand shifts to the back of my head and he holds me there, firmly but not tightly.

"That's it, gorgeous, hold me there. Make me feel good. Keep me nice and hard so I can give you what you need. Suck at it, Nigh."

I struggle to obey, breathing minimally through my nose, feeling my throat muscles pulse and flutter around the large intruder. I tighten my lips around his cock and try to generate some form of suction, but it's difficult. I moan in frustration, wanting to please and hating to fail.

"That's good, baby, you feel so good, you are so good. I'm gonna pull out now, OK? You stay still."

He slowly withdraws his cock from my throat, saliva and pre-cum spilling over my bottom lip. Rylan swipes a finger over a droplet. "Oops, baby, you don't want to waste this," he teases as I lick away the liquid, "although I do like seeing you literally drooling for my dick. You need it bad, don't you, baby?"

I nod again, feeling desperate, and opening my mouth, showing him how good I am, how useful.

He chuckles and happily slides his cock into my mouth again. "Good, Nigh, swallow it down. I want your throat so full of cock that your voice goes hoarse. That way every time you say a word I will picture you just like this." He fucks my mouth a little faster, before pulling out suddenly and slapping my cheek with his cock. "That's enough, slut, I don't want to come just yet and your pretty little face is making me want to do just that. Would you like that? My cum coating your face so all you could do was taste it, smell it, feel it?"

My own cock throbs and aches with want and I wonder if it's possible to get off from words alone.

"Well?" he prods, and I realize he wants an answer.

I don't think I know one until I realize I've already opened my mouth and the words are spilling out. "I want anything you want to give me."

"God, you're perfect," Rylan breathes and then swats me unexpectedly on the back of the head. "Living room. Crawl. Now."

It's weird, because even though I have a roommate and Rylan lives alone, we almost never spend time here. The old carpet is rough under my hands and knees and Rylan slaps my ass—hard—as I scuttle awkwardly forward.

"Good," he says, when I reach the open space between the couch and television. He grabs me none-too-gently by the hair and pulls me onto my knees, yanking my head back. He shoves two salty fingers in my mouth, then four. It's a brutal assault and my lips spread uncomfortably over his skin. His fingertips jab at my soft palate. "You were good, baby, but you can still be better for me, can't you? I don't wanna have to go gentle on you. I wanna fuck your mouth whenever I want, however I want and as hard as I want. That understood?" he tells me, his voice calm and his fingers reckless.

I try to nod with a mouthful of knuckles. I feel useless and stupid and I want to do better. I suck hard at his fingers—frantic to show him how good I can be. It's pathetic and absurd and addictive and it fires arousal through me. I reach desperately for my neglected and fraught erection.

Rylan snaps his hand out of my mouth and smacks my arm away. He uses his vicious hold on my hair to jerk me forward. I collapse onto my hands and knees. He kicks my thighs apart, exposing me, and dips two saliva-wet fingers into my anus, thrusting them back and forth idly for a minute.

"Don't move," he orders, withdrawing his hand and giving my ass cheek another couple of solid, opened-handed blows. I hear him leave and shuffle around for something in his room. I can't see anything with my head pressed against the rough carpet and my ass squirms pathetically, seeking out something that isn't there.

Rylan returns, and with him comes a saccharine mandarin-orange smell. For a moment I can't identify it, but when I feel his decisively lubed fingers spread my ass and enter me, I remember.

"You're fucking kidding me, Ry," I manage to get out, the smell dragging me out of oblivion.

"Shut up," he laughs, working a couple of fingers into my asshole. "You never come over, so this is the only stuff I've got here." It's cheap, scented/flavoured lube that I bought by accident when we were first starting out. It wasn't as though I'd thought it would be a particularly good idea. It was more that I was so embarrassed to be in a sex store, and so terrified that they would ask to see my ID, which stated very obviously that I was sixteen, that I had grabbed the first lube I'd found, turned bright red, paid, and ran. We'd only used it once or twice, before Rylan subtly replaced it with something that didn't smell like sugary chemicals.

"Are you sure it isn't expired or something?" I ask, finding myself not all that deterred and greedily pushing back into him.

"Not until next month, I checked," he replies. "Now shut up, would you?"

I happily oblige, revelling in the feel of his fingers as they crook and tease inside me. He slides his knuckles up the muscles to either side of my spine and then digs his fingers into the top of my shoulders, disallowing me from moving forward and away—as if I would want to.

He adds another finger and I feel the delicious burn as I widen to accommodate him.

"Good," he murmurs appreciatively, and his thumb rubs my neck where it holds me in place. He seeks out my prostate and runs his fingertips over it. I buck needfully as pleasure zings through me. God, I want him.

"Oh, you want to be fucked, Nigh Uncanny?" he enquires, mock surprise colouring his voice.

I whine petulantly in response and shimmy my ass against his knuckles, trying to get them impossibly deeper.

"Tell you what," Rylan continues, sliding his hand up over my neck and onto the back of my head. He applies pressure. "You put your face down and your ass up like a little bitch in heat, and I'll see what we can do for you."

I obey almost mindlessly, pressing my face to the scratchy carpet and shoving my hips up further. I brace myself, pressing my palms into the ground beside my shoulders. I feel his warm cockhead slide along my ass crack, pausing over my hole, and then sliding lower. I bite back another protesting murmur. His cock slides back up, and just as I think he's going to enter, he pulls back.

"You know what?" he contemplates, his tone smooth and cruel. "I think if you want my cock so bad, you should help me out, open yourself up."

For a second I don't comprehend his meaning; and then I do, and my hands fly backwards, scrabbling for purchase and spreading my ass cheeks wide, as if I would do anything to get him to fuck me. My skin burns in shame at how quickly I respond to his request and he runs a solitary finger around the inner, corrugated edge of my anus. I feel it twitch wantonly at him and that only makes me blush hotter and my dick harder.

"Here?" he teases.

"Uh huh," I murmur.

"Speak up, Niles. I can't hear you."

"Yes," I whisper.

He smacks my ass. "I said louder." The words are taut and certain.

"Please," I answer, my voice shaky but loud. "Please fuck me, please fuck my ass. Please, Ry. I want it. I want it so fucking badly, please just—"

Anything else I have to say is cut off as his cock enters me with one ruthless thrust. I grunt in response. The momentum causes my face to skid forward along the carpet. My hands fly off my ass as I struggle to maintain my position. Rylan grabs at me, his fingertips biting into my lower ribs as he wrenches me back towards him, seating his cock even deeper within me.

"This what you wanted, baby?" he demands, accentuating his meaning with driving thrusts. I emit a little groan and he answers back with a satisfied, guttural noise of his own, sketching his nails over my ribs and under me, where they painfully bite at the skin on my thighs.

His movements lessen in depth but not in intensity as he violently slams into me. I brace myself staunchly and twist so that my forehead is now pressed against the floor as if in prayer. I keen into the carpet, my jaw opening to allow animalistic sounds to escape. I'm so turned on that my breath comes out in short, hollow pants between sobs. I inventory the multiple pain points in my body: dull, positional pain in my wrists; a throbbing ache in my knees from where they jam against the hostile carpet-covered cement; sharp, stinging pain in my thighs; and the terse stretch of my asshole as Rylan fucks into me. He bites my shoulder and I add that sudden stab to my list.

Even in the moment I can't quite comprehend why this so, so does it for me. Rylan is still ignoring my dick, and he pounds into me so quickly that I can barely concentrate on the flashes of pleasure that mix in along with agonizing discomfort. But it does do it for me. Knowing the rug below me is old and filthy;

that I spread myself for him; that I sucked and slobbered for this: that I am getting what I both deserve and begged for—

Rylan changes the angle of his thrusts suddenly, and it jolts me. He grabs a fistful of my hair, rubbing my face into the carpet like a naughty dog. If I were to twist and look back, I could catch sight of my straining, leaking cock.

"Touch it," Rylan orders, and, even though I barely have the strength to support us both on one arm, I scramble to encircle my cock with my hand, stroking it furiously. "And while you come, you'll thank me," Rylan instructs. "Just because you're orgasming doesn't mean you can forget your manners."

I don't know if it's my grip or his condescending, shaming tone but almost instantly I'm coming, spattering jism all over the spiteful carpet and my own chest. "Thank you," I'm panting. "Thank you for fucking me." I want to sink to the floor with relief but Rylan isn't done. He wraps one arm roughly around my waist and fucks me hard and fast until he's unloading into me. I can feel him, hot and wet inside of my squandered body.

His arm remains clamped around me for probably a full minute, maybe longer, before he slowly pulls out and away. I allow myself to tip sideways and off of my tortured knees. I can feel his cum seeping out of my abused asshole and I don't care. Rylan comes to rest nearby; he drops his head onto my thigh.

"You should probably buy me some kneepads if you're in the mood to do that ever again," I say, finally. "Also I officially hate this carpet."

"Oh, you loved every filthy second of it," Rylan quips.

I sigh. "Yes. Yes, I did."

"Shower?" he suggests.

"Please."

He drags me upwards by the forearms and pulls me along by the hand, the nasty orange smell trailing after our sweaty bodies.

- 13 -

"So, Captain," Rylan is saying after we've finally dragged ourselves away from the shower, and tidied up the carpet. "As nice as that was, I do actually want to know what's up."

He pushes me gently onto the couch and straddles my lap, hands linked casually behind my neck.

"I don't know," I offer, quasi-hopefully.

He raises a skeptical eyebrow.

"Just something Shona said," I acknowledge, uncomfortably.

He cocks his head to one side, intimating for me to continue.

"Do you..." I don't quite know how to phrase what I'm asking. I don't even know if I know what I want to ask. "Do you think this is normal?"

"Do I think what is normal?"

"Us?" I practically swallow the word but he still seems to hear me.

"Niles." He sounds amused. "Darling. Don't be ridiculous."

"What?!" I blush and dip my head, trying to escape his knowing eye contact.

"Of course this isn't normal!" He laughs, and crooks a knuckle under my chin. "First off, we're both dudes. So we're basically saying, 'Fuck heteronormativity.' Which is kind of status quo. So by that alone we're—quote-unquote—abnormal. On top of that, in case you haven't noticed, we've got just a titch of a sub-Dom thing going on...and while that's not all that wild and unheard of, so far as kinks go, it's probably not what people would classify as vanilla. So, no, babe, I'd say we're decisively not normal."

"Stupid question, hey?" I allow a smile.

He kisses me. "A bit, but I won't tell anyone." He studies my face, "Nigh? Just because we're not...normal doesn't mean what we have isn't...good...you know? I mean...you like it, right?"

I nod, easily, because it's the truth.

"And I like it," Rylan continues, "and you, like, trust that I would never ever do anything where I don't feel like I know what I'm doing?"

I start to speak. It would be so easy just to agree, to sink back into the safety of him, but I know I can't.

"I—I wish I did. I want to."

Worry clouds his face. "What do you mean?"

I swallow, hard. "The choking thing," I reply.

He rubs his thumb over my cheek. "I was counting the whole time in my head. If you hadn't come by the time I got to one hundred and twenty, I would've stopped."

"I didn't know that."

"You weren't supposed to know that," he answers, smiling. "You were just supposed to get off."

"And I did," I assure him hurriedly. "It's just that, Ry, you were wasted. Or maybe not wasted. but definitely drunk. and I just...I just think it was kind of shitty of you to spring that on me when I didn't know where you were at, like, drunk-wise."

Rylan looks like he's going to argue—his eyebrows furrow and he rolls off of me and crosses his arms over his body. I know he feels rejected and I did that and I can't stand it.

"I'm sorry," I say, suddenly. "I shouldn't've brought it up. It's old news and—"

Rylan turns back towards me, and covers my mouth with a couple of fingers. "Stop, Niles, are you fucking kidding me?"

There's no malice in his words, only wonder. "I do something that literally makes you afraid of me and you're *apologizing*? Jesus, baby. I'm the one who is sorry. You're right. Of course you're right. I didn't think of it like that because I felt so good, so in control and I saw how it was affecting you—or at least I thought I did."

He draws towards me and presses his forehead against my cheek. "I'm so sorry," he says, quietly, earnestly. "That was so horrifically stupid of me and I swear to God I'll try never to fuck up like that again."

I nod and grip his hand. My eyes burn and I didn't know I could feel this relieved. "Thank you," I whisper. He squeezes my hand back.

"I like to think I know what I'm doing, especially when it comes to you, but I guess I don't, and I hate that."

"Yeah, but you do like ninety-eight percent of the time, so I think you're alright."

"OK," he replies, and there's an unfamiliar note of sadness in his voice. "I'm seriously sorry and I love you, OK?"

"I love you, too," I reply, quietly.

We breathe together for a moment.

"God, that orange shit still stinks up the place," Rylan says, to ease the silence. "When did you buy it again?"

"Just after the third time we had sex."

He smiles slyly at me. "Remember the first time?"

"You mean do I remember the first time you had sex on me, in Julie Upperman's basement?" He had, too—waited 'til everyone else had passed out drunk, pushed me down, sucked me hard and climbed on my dick, right next to the washer and dryer.

"I wanted to show you it wouldn't hurt," he protests.

I crack up completely. "You're kidding! You looked like you were gonna die the whole time. I could barely get off!"

125

"How was I supposed to know saliva is shitty lubrication?"

"Oh, I don't know. The internet, maybe?"

"Oh. Right," Rylan replies. He blushes and I bite his chin, playfully. "Guess that's another example of me not getting it right."

"Yeah," I agree. "But thankfully for both of us, you learn from your mistakes."

* * *

I take the summer off school. I was planning on going back for a couple of courses, but I figure as this is going to be pretty much the only time pre-retirement that I can sort of justify not working that I might as well. My parents are still so freaked about the Kya thing that they are being super generous and affectionate and seem legitimately happy to keep paying my bills. Rylan tells me I'm spoiled as fuck and I wholly acknowledge this.

In penance, I spend a lot of time over at my parents' house, hanging out with Kya and, when she's around, Matilda. We do dorky-fun local things: ride the little, green, inner-harbour ferries; visit the bug emporium; eat shitty, over-priced gelato. When Rylan's not working, he tags along. Or, more, I tag along with them. It's like they have a secret language, one odd noise accompanied with a ridiculous facial expression from Rylan sends Kya into peals of giggles, while I stand nearby, oblivious and dog-paddling between jealousy and adoration.

People stare a lot, and not at Rylan and me. Every once in a while, of course, some stupid redneck tourists will give us a glare, but honestly we get more encouraging smiles than anything else. I sometimes think they think maybe Kya's our kid? Mostly it's not about the gay PDA thing, though. I think the curious glances are at Kya and her sequined eye-patch.

Most people think it's a costume or something and people behind counters and at ice cream stands love to smile and say, "Oooh, a pirate!" or, more often, "Now, why are you hiding one of those beautiful brown eyes?"

Kya, of course, thinks that the best way to address this is just to flip up her patch and expose the green, plastic comforter that fills the socket, and grin. This is awkward as fuck, causing people to blush, and apologize profusely, which in turn makes me blush and apologize profusely and hiss, "Kya!" which Rylan says I shouldn't do, because it's not her fault people are rude enough to ask.

Today, Shona is coming along on our daily adventure. Kya is bringing one of her friends. Everyone shows up at my parents' house around eleven. Kya's friend's mother hands me an EpiPen.

"Cara can't have peanuts, walnuts, pecans, cashews, bananas, eggs or wheat!" she spouts, and I decide right then and there that we aren't eating today. I refuse to purchase a single edible thing, because there is no way I am being responsible for inserting a needle into a young girl's thigh. Not gonna happen. So, fasting it is. Rylan joins us on the driveway just as we are about to climb into the car.

"What are you doing here?" I demand. "I thought you had to work."

"Bathroom flooded. Had to close shop." He grins.

"Oh really? And just what did you flush in order to arrange that?" I ask.

He looks scandalized. "Just how terrible a person do you think I am!?"

Before I have a chance to answer, Kya catapults herself onto Rylan's back. Shona shrieks in reaction because all of us, including Shona and excluding Kya, are blatantly terrified of Kya injuring herself as a result of her recent loss of depth perception. Rylan manages to adjust though, flinging his hands under her knees. He makes a sound like a trumpet, and continues into a few bars of some song I don't recognize, but that Kya seems to know, because she finishes it off with him. Cara stares.

Kya scrambles awkwardly up Rylan's back until she's perched on his shoulders, and he marches over to me. Kya forms huge claws with her arms.

"NILES CLARENCE RUTEBAKER!" she wails menacingly. "WE ARE GOING TO EAT YOU UP!"

"Clarence," Rylan snorts. "I need to remember that more often." He kisses me squarely on the mouth, while Kya's hand-claws attack my hair. "Itinerary, Captain," he commands, lowering a reluctant Kya onto the cement.

"Petting zoo, followed by walk along the breakwater, followed by one of those downtown horse-drawn carriage tour things."

Rylan whistles. "Who's doling out the big bucks?"

"Mom and Dad!" Kya announces.

"Spoiled much?" Rylan counters.

I blush. "Almost to the point of decay," I answer, but I feel awkward. I know I am, or at least my family is, a lot more well-off than Rylan. I just don't know what to do about it.

"Decrepit. You know what I like, Alberta," Rylan laughs and licks my cheek. "Mmmm...fetid flesh. So good right now."

Cara looks stunned.

"Christ, you guys. Children and necrophilia don't mix," Shona cuts in. "Let's get going, shall we?"

"What's necra...feelings?" Cara lisps hesitantly.

"Um. It's a...dangerous...animal. That you shouldn't pet," I offer, weakly, fighting with Kya to buckle her seatbelt.

"No it isn't!" Kya argues, bright eye fixed accusingly on me, "It's when a guy puts his thi—"

"KYA!" Shona and I collectively shut her up. Rylan cracks up.

"C'mon, Trooper. There is plenty of time to discuss that in, say, twelve years. But right now, if you value Cara's friendship, you'll keep it a secret," he says, conspiratorially. Kya looks slightly disappointed, but doesn't fill her friend in on the sad facts of life (or death?), thank goodness. If she did, the EpiPen would be the least of my worries.

* * *

"Nigh," Rylan says to me as we stand against the fence at the petting zoo, watching Kya and Cara feeding the baby goats and squealing. "I want to ask you something and I don't want you to answer right now, but I want you to know I'm thinking about it and I want you to think about it, too."

"Um. OK..." I answer, looking at him sideways. Rylan snakes his hand around the small of my back, oblivious to the mothers standing awkwardly by, watching while trying to pretend they aren't. He leans his face in close to mine. He grins, then kisses me, perhaps a little more heartily than is decent for a local children's attraction. He pulls back, his eyes lighting on my mouth before swooping up to my face.

"OK, good. It's this: do you think we should have a safe word?"

Whatever I was expecting, it was not that, but I don't even have to time to think, let alone reply, before Kya bounces up to us, face wind-whipped and bright.

"Niles, we're bored," she announces.

"You weren't bored thirty seconds ago! I saw you hanging with that fat goat."

"Her name is Pearl," Kya corrects me. "And I'm bored. And hungry."

"We're fasting today," I reply immediately. Rylan gives me a confused look. "What? I don't want to feed Cara anything she's allergic to," I justify.

"I'll cover it," Shona says, walking up to us, one hand holding Cara's and the other wiping sawdust off on her jean shorts. "Don't worry."

"OK." I hesitate. "If you're sure. I am very anti-anaphylaxis."

"It'll be fine," she promises.

"Thank you," I reply, grateful to be relieved of responsibility. "Kids are terrifying and stressful and should be avoided."

"Good thing you don't have a uterus, then, I guess," Shona replies. "Careful with the gate, girls. We don't want any runaway goats."

* * *

After lunch we walk the sea wall, and then climb over rocks and driftwood, down to the pebbly beach, where Rylan races ahead with Cara and Kya, dashing in and out of the surf. The three rescue tubular kelp from the ocean and then proceed to squish the round, rubbery heads firmly underfoot. They hoot and screech and then repeat.

I squint out, watching them. Shona seems to have chosen lunch wisely—Cara is in no apparent distress.

Shona's looking at me, with a strange sort of smile on her face.

"What?" I ask, feeling my face heat up slightly.

She shrugs. "You look happy."

"So?"

"So, I don't know. I just think it's nice."

"What's nice?"

"You. And Rylan. You just seem…happy. It's nice."

"Alright. Weirdo." I nudge her gently with my shoulder. She looks back at me through giant, red polka-dotted sunglasses.

"I still don't really get the monogamy thing," she elaborates.

I raise an eyebrow. "So, Jesse, he was just, what? A year and a half of faking it?"

"No!" Shona backpedals. "I mean, technically, I never cheated on him. I mean, we broke up a lot, so I hooked up with other people when we were being broken up, but never when we were actually together."

Oh. "I didn't know that."

Shona shrugs. "It's not something I'm, you know, proud of. I just figured that was the way people are. Like, can anyone really be faithful to someone for a lifetime? Like in forty years, am I going to want to be looking at the same old dick? Is my life going to devolve into a series of, 'Did you turn off the outside lights?' and, 'Pack me a lunch, would you, sweetheart?' like my parents?"

"I don't know. Is that so terrible? I mean, my folks have been together for a long time—and I guess there is routine, but they also seem to genuinely like each other. And then there's other stuff, like support? Like when we were going through the thing with Kya it seemed almost like it brought my parents closer?"

"Yeah," Shona vaguely agrees, "but yours and my parents are like, some of the only couples I know who are still together after a decade. And that's supposedly the best case scenario? Like figuring out whose turn it is to empty the dishwasher or take out the compost? Is that really it for us?"

"I guess. I don't know." She might be right. I've never wanted to think of the life my parents built as depressingly mundane, but it isn't exactly extraordinary, either, but then again, it's safe, and easy and—happy. "So, you don't want to...be with someone? Like, permanently?" I ask. "Not that I'm judging, I'm just curious."

"I don't know," she sighs. "Maybe I'm still reeling from the whole Jesse catastrophe, but even when I was with him I always had an eye out, trying to see if I had, I dunno, better prospects or something."

"Huh," I reply, genuinely surprised.

"Well, don't you? Maybe not have an eye out, exactly—sorry. I guess that's a shitty choice in words. I mean, don't you ever even wonder what it would be like with someone else? If the sex would be better, or another guy would complement your strengths and weaknesses better, or I dunno, he was taller than you? And I'm not trying to bash Rylan here, because it seems like you guys are finally figuring shit out and you know I'm happy so long as you're happy. Just don't you ever daydream, even briefly, about a different guy, a different relationship?"

I think about it. But, really, if I'm completely honest... "No."

"Seriously?"

"I don't. I mean. I think about what things would be like if *our* relationship was better. Like if I was better at saying what I'm thinking, or we'd been more clear when we'd first started out. I mean, to be fair I've been so preoccupied with terror that I've had it all wrong all this time—like, fixated on whether *he* wanted me or not, to the point of not even thinking of alternatives. But, I dunno. He's what I want."

"Monogamy. Weird. I don't know, Nigh. I don't think most people are like you, in their heart of hearts. I think most people are more opportunistic."

"Do you mean you think Rylan is more opportunistic?" I challenge.

132

"Jesus, I did not mean that and I am so not even touching that. Do not even try to pass your insecurities off on me, got it?"

"Yeah," I concede. "Sorry. I need to stop doing that."

"You don't need to do anything, Niles, for any*one*. Not unless you genuinely want to. That's kind of the point. C'mon. Let's get our feet wet."

I accept the segue and balance on one foot to take off my shoes. Shona follows suit. We walk along barefoot through the mud, and she takes my hand and I know we're good.

Cara runs up to us, stares at us, suspiciously, and runs away again.

* * *

Cara, it turns out, is both confused and not very good at being secretive. To be fair, she's only eight. It's the end of the carriage ride and we're all disembarking, heading back to the car. Rylan is bounding ahead, inexhaustible. Cara and Kya are walking just in front of Shona and me. Cara is whispering very loudly.

"Kya, I have to tell you something," Cara states decisively, like she's been dying to say this all day and has just summoned the courage and there is no way of going back on her word now.

"What?" Kya interrogates. "Is it a secret? Is it good?"

Cara glances conspicuously at Shona and me. "I think your brother is not a very good boyfriend. He's holding hands with that girl, again, but I saw him kiss that man," she motions furtively to Rylan, "six times today, and one time my mom saw her boyfriend holding hands with a girl at ShopMore and she said it made him a bad boyfriend."

"Oh," Kya replies, giving in to the beautiful simplicity of kid logic. "I don't think you're right though, because I think if Niles was being a bad boyfriend he probably would try to be sneakier about it."

Cara nods, sagely. "You're probably right. Martin looked reeeeeeeeeally surprised to see me and Mom."

Rylan stops and turns and grins. "You know, Kya, you are smart as shit."

Cara looks nonplussed. "The sh-word is smart?" she asks.

- 14 -

Even though I promised not to let them, the things Shona said are really niggling at me. She's right—most of our friends' parents are divorced. Rylan's parents are divorced...well, more like, never together, and I guess I've always known that monogamy isn't exactly problem free, or even the only model for relationships. Then again, he said he'd never cheat on me and I'm trying really hard to do this "trusting Rylan" thing these days.

"So? You think about what I asked?" Rylan says, kissing my ear. We're mostly naked in my bed at home and he's been trying to fuck me all morning.

Besides what Shona said, I've been thinking about not a lot else.

I shake him off, glaring at the computer open on my lap. "I guess. Give me a minute. I'm trying to pick my courses."

He closes his eyes and points to a spot on the page. "Do that one."

"Acquiring Expert Venture Cognitions," I read. "How did you know?"

He laughs and drops his face to between my laptop and my groin. He uses his nose to scrunch up the leg of my boxers and presses his mouth softly against my upper thigh, before responding, "Entrepreneurship not your thing. Got it. I don't mean to be a nag, Captain, but aren't you sort of supposed to have a major by now?"

"I think I have one!" I protest. "Maybe! I think geography?"

But my brain is distracted—back to stupid Shona-inspired insecurities. Maybe I'm being selfish. Maybe by assuming this is a long term thing, I'm almost trapping Rylan into something that doesn't fit. Maybe this isn't right for him. He's so great with kids, like maybe he wants some of his own someday to replace his kind of shitty family and while great for now, somewhere down the line there are such big chunks of his history that I think I should know, but don't, and maybe if I just had more information, I could figure this shit out.

"Have you seen your mom, lately?" I blurt out, obtusely.

Rylan doesn't move for a long moment, and then slowly sits up. "No," he replies, carefully, "What brought that on?"

"I don't know," I say apologetically. I know I shouldn't bring shit like that up. I just...I feel like he's got an unfair advantage. He knows where I come from, who my family is, and how he fits with them and maybe I want that, too. Like they might be fuck-ups, but they're still his family, right?

I can tell he's thinking but I can't tell what. He shifts to face me. "How come you never just tell me what you mean?" he presses, quietly, non-accusingly, even though God knows I deserve to be accused. I know he's trying to be gentle with me, to keep me calm, but the question still makes my stomach drop and my pulse hopscotch. I wish he wouldn't because maybe I just don't want to do the talking thing after all. Maybe it's too hard.

"I don't know," I wheedle. I'm trying to worm out of the whole situation and I know it and I hate it. I try to distract myself with the UVic calendar again, but Rylan simply removes it from my hands, closes it, and puts it on the bedside table. He kisses the side of my neck with a patience I don't deserve.

"Tell me, please," he states. He doesn't beg.

"I don't know what to tell you!" I exclaim.

"Start with a little part." His voice is low and formidable. He slinks around behind me so he's sitting, legs splayed, between the headboard and my back and runs his hands up and down my sides. He pulls me into him. "You don't even have to look at me. Just give me something, OK?"

"Something of what?"

"Don't deflect," he demands, his voice slightly sharper.

I sigh and his fingers encircle my naked waist.

"Nothing." I insist, and he bites my shoulder, hard. "Something Shona said."

He laps at the wound he just created, kisses it. "Jesus Christ. That woman." He continues his attentions, trailing lips and tongue up my neck, fingertips scouting the area around my navel.

"I'm sorry," I offer, mulishly.

"Keep going." He nips at my ear. "What did she say?"

"Just stuff."

He sinks his teeth into the back of my neck, quite possibly breaking the skin.

"Fuck, Ry! That hurts!"

"Then stop delaying the inevitable." His teeth poise on the verge of attack.

"Look. I just worry, OK?"

I can picture his smirk, even though his face is behind me, as he says, "Tell me something I don't know." Then his voice softens. "Seriously, Niles, what is it I don't know?"

He kisses my cheek, slides his hand over my stomach and ribs.

"Are you happy?" I ask, finally.

"Yes. Very." His answer is fluid, confident.

I inhale. "Me too. Like. Really happy." There. That was progress, right?

"Good." He plucks at a nipple, causing my dick to take interest.

"And you—you think we'll keep being happy for…" I trail off, uselessly.

"The foreseeable future." He slides a hand into my shorts and takes my cock in his hand. The warmth of his palm elicits the expected reaction and he rearranges my erection so it's in typical jack-off position.

"Right," I breathe.

His hand tightens gently and then relaxes rhythmically around my cock—no real intention present. I'd accuse him of not listening, but I know he is—and intently. He presses his lips to my temple, my jaw. His free hand skates over the skin on my inner thigh, promising to stroke my balls before maddeningly withdrawing. I lean against him, wanting. I don't know how to react to the talking and the touching at the same time, and I'm guessing that's his game plan.

"So, why the philosophizing?" he continues. I bite my lip as he squeezes my erection this side of too hard—just the way I like it.

"Just thinking." And suddenly he's gone, and I fall back, or he pushes me, and he's over me, straddling my lap.

"Talk to me, Niles. For fuck's sake." He holds my cheeks in his hands.

"I don't know how," I whisper.

"Yes, you do. Start small. What are you happy, with?" he prompts. He slots our cocks together, the fabric between us generating a painful-pleasant friction, and grips my wrists, confining them to the bedspread.

"My family." It feels beyond bizarre to be talking about my family like this, but it's what he wants, what he told me to do. "The fact that Kya's OK, that I'm going back to school and I maybe even found something I want to pursue."

Rylan drags his hips along, parallel to mine. "Good, baby, you're doing so good," he whispers into the skin beneath my jaw.

Suddenly my hands are shoved upwards against the wall—caught by one of Rylan's small hands and my own determination to obey—and he bites or kisses at my throat. His praise punches through me like an arrow, exhilarating everything: my breath, my pulse, my arousal. "My friends. My apartment," I continue, like a mantra.

He plunges the heel of his free hand upwards, hard over the skin of my chest, and then runs his nails downwards. Until I say it.

Until what I say I know is true. "You."

His lips find mine, his tongue strong and demanding, and my cock is responding to him, I'm rocking my hips up into him. He lets my hands go and I grasp onto him, arms reckless around his neck.

"And what are you worried about?" he urges, knowing that by this point, I can't resist. I shake my head, but he catches my lip between his teeth, stilling me immediately. Slamming his hips against mine, he lets me feel that I am not alone in this.

"Going back to school," I whisper. "Knowing like I do now that shitty things can happen to me, even if I've always pretended they can't."

"And?" The pace is faster now. He uses one hand to grip me by the hair on the back of my head and I grasp wildly at his biceps, trying to steady us, which is impossible and I know it.

"And...being out. I try not to let people get to me, but—"

"It happens, and you handle it beautifully and stoically and I'm so fucking proud of you," he tells me and I swear to God I can actually hear his love and it is so much bigger than me and I want it so much—

"What else, sweetness?" he prompts, finally lowering his hand to fully encircle my aching cock. I try to name more but all I can think about is him as we slide together. He strokes me evenly, deftly, and it's my turn to grab his head, slamming it down towards mine because I need somewhere to put the noises I'm making, but he won't let me. His lips tease at mine, disallowing any substantial pressure. I'm trying to be quiet, trying to muffle myself, even though I know there's no one around to hear us.

"For God's sake, Nigh," he whispers. "Say it. Scream it if you have to."

No. I shake my head.

"Scream."

I can't help it. It's an order.

So I do. It's low and hoarse and ugly, but he demands it of me again and I'm so close to coming I can't argue, I can only submit.

"And—" he dictates, a final time and it's not even a question anymore. "What the fucking hell are you so worried about?"

And I whimper. But then I say it. Scream it. Come.

"You."

* * *

I refuse to open my eyes. If I open my eyes I have to face it: The Conversation. If I keep them closed I can just lie here forever, never having to talk about anything, ever again.

But if Rylan's anything, it's patient, or maybe just stubborn. Either way, he can outlast my forever, anytime.

He's still straddling me. My dick is softening quickly, his hand still wrapped around it. It's weird. There's cum, and my sweat, and my throat is sore.

140

Finally, he releases me and I feel him wiping us up with maybe a T-shirt and the simple hominess of the gesture makes me feel oddly cared for. Fuck. His hand touches my face, and I flinch slightly, caught off-guard. He shifts forward. I know the kiss is coming before it touches my lips. And it's patient, too, of course.

"Niles," he says, softly. I want to turn my head away, but I don't move. I'm not acknowledging this. I'm waiting for him to get bored and go home.

Instead, he preciously strips me of my boxer shorts, rummages through the drawers and passes me a clean pair, along with a T-shirt. I numbly dress myself, while he kicks off his boxers, erection not yet waned. He doesn't bother dressing, instead gently observing me. He takes his time, afterwards, straightens the fabric under his hands, finger-combs my hair. I feel his palms slide down my torso, pausing on my hip bones. He curls up, naked, beside me and tucks his head under my chin.

"Niles," he repeats.

He's not going anywhere.

I cover my eyes with my palms. Surrender.

"Sit up," he instructs, half-coaxing and half-telling, but I let my hands fall and manoeuvre my body up to lean against the headboard. He falls into place next to me, copying my posture, knees up, fingers clasped over them. But he's looking at me and not at the sheets. Waiting again.

"This is hard," I say, finally, my voice scratchy in my throat.

"Shouldn't be," he says, seeming to take my words as a cue to touch me, because his hand slips behind my back and I half-wish he wouldn't. I can't concentrate on anything but him when he does.

"At least when we weren't talking I knew what to obsess about."

He snorts gently, but doesn't reply.

"Now it's just…Everything is supposed to be all fine and stuff, but if I start to think too much about something then I have to ask it, but for some reason the asking is just terrifying. Even though logically it shouldn't be. I've just never been taught to talk like this."

He looks at me strangely.

"You've forgotten," he says.

I glance at him sideways. "What?"

"Even when we weren't acknowledging this out loud, or even now that we are—we're still best friends, Nigh. Nothing's changed in that regard. And we never had any problems talking before."

"Except about us," I counter. But he's right, of course. How the hell can I feel uncomfortable around Rylan when he's already privy to every last thing about me?

He sighs. "I'm still sorry. You know that, right? I should've figured it out that you didn't want to say anything earlier, because then we wouldn't have this three-year-cloud hanging over us, making everything a million times more difficult."

I feel myself relax involuntarily. Of course he'd take the blame. "Yeah," I agree. "All you needed to do was learn how to read my mind."

He laughs. "Or you mine. Whatever, though. We're dealing with it now, right?"

"Yeah," I agree again. "And I just—I want you to know that I'm pretty, like…invested."

"And Shona says that's weird? For you to be invested in me? I mean, we've invested three years, so I kind of thought it was a given." Rylan shakes his head. "Why is she so set upon fucking you up?"

"Hey. She's only heard my tortured side of our story for all this time. She's defensive for a reason."

142

"And I appreciate her being there for you, but seriously, she has got to give me a chance to be the good guy. What did she say? Did she say I'd screw around on you?"

"No," I answer truthfully.

"Did she say I'd walk out on you?"

"No."

"Then I don't get it."

"She said—" God, now it sounds so stupid. "She said most people aren't, like, as fiercely monogamous as me." I blush. Monogamous. What an eighth grade, family-life kind of word.

Rylan shakes his head. "Of course she did," he says under his breath. He doesn't say anything more, so I force myself to end my misery and ask.

"Well?"

"Well," Rylan responds, "I guess there's no way around it. She's right. I can't think of a single other person on Earth that is interested in finding another person that they might just be into. Security and love, and having someone to go home to— kill me now." His sarcasm is deafening, but he just steamrolls right on. "I mean, look at us idiots. What have we even been doing? Three fucking years wasted in a monogamous relationship, when we could have been out having vanilla sex with sloppy, drunk strangers. I don't know about you, babe, but I totally feel like I'm missing out on all those things I never wanted."

"Gotcha. So we're good," I say, blushing with one part relief and one part embarrassment.

"Good," he repeats. "Great, fantastic. You hear me?"

I nod and he kisses me and we sit there quietly for a while.

"Nigh?" he says, after a while.

"Mmm?"

"The safe word thing? Since we're talking?"

143

I force myself not to fall into another shame spiral. "I..." I clear my throat. "I've actually been thinking about it a lot," I say. "And, I think, I think if it's OK, I'd rather we don't."

Rylan nods, thoughtfully. "Alright. Can I ask why?"

"Yeah, um, look, I've done some reading online and stuff, and I know that we're supposed to have one and stuff, but I just don't want one. I would rather just be able to trust that when I say 'stop' you will. But mostly I think it is because, as you might have noticed, I'm not super good with the words in general, and I think if I had to say a weird, random word during sex, I would feel so weird about it that I just wouldn't use it. Whereas with stop, it's like—a conversation opener. Stop what? Stop how? Does this hurt? Do you want to keep going? I dunno—am I making any sense?"

"Lots and lots," he promises. "Stop it is. The other thing is—do you want to talk, like, boundaries? Like things you like or things you're into or things you're definitely not into."

"I don't know," I reply, slowly.

"You don't have to answer now. Just thought I'd bring it up—I've been doing a bit of reading of my own, since the—you know, our last talk."

"No, I think I can answer now—I, err, how do I put this? OK. Like, again, I know there is kind of a 'right way' to do this, where we like, I dunno, make and swap lists or something, or discuss what's going to play out before it happens and—I know I should want that—it's safe. But—I just don't. I don't want to know what's coming. I don't want to say stuff I will or will not do, because what I want the most is to—Jesus—it's to do what you want, to take what you give, to accept it and not question it."

"Christ, Nigh. You're making me hard."

"Yeah?"

144

"Fuck, yes. God, the idea of you so willing and wanting and generous—it's beautiful."

"I want to trust you not to give me more than I can handle, even if what I think I can handle and what you think I can handle are two different things."

"God, I want that so much," Rylan says, petting my hair and kissing my face. "I mean, you can change your mind and just tell me if you wanna discuss something, but fuck, I love surprising you and pushing you and stretching you and making you so, so mine."

"I want that," I say. "But I'm not there yet, exactly. I—I'm not sure how I'd react if we tried the choking thing again. I seriously can't think of anything else I wouldn't happily, willingly take from you if you thought it best—and I know that's fucked up, but it's also true—but I'm not ready for that."

"For sure. Yes. Of course. I won't go there. Not now, not ever if you don't want, OK?"

"Yeah. OK. Thank you," I say.

Rylan laughs. "Yes, you're so welcome for giving me unmitigated access to your body."

"Say that again and I'll be hard. Jesus."

"Un-mit-i-gat-ed ac-cess," he says, his lips moving obscenely with every syllable. "Mine to fuck when I want to, where I want to and *if* I want to—"

I maybe whine a little bit.

"Fuck, babe. I love you so much and you are so, so good for me."

"Thank you," I whisper.

"Now, bend over the side of this bed and prove it."

I've never moved so goddamn fast.

- 15 -

School: my very relaxed summer made me forget how much *time* it takes up. Hanging around the university centre to get my ID validated; waiting in line for literally an hour and a half to get my textbooks, and now, first day of classes. The majority of my profs just read aloud from the class syllabus, because most of us (myself included) won't read it if they don't. This makes for short classes, but a dry, dull day that I can't wait to be over, because I have plans to hang out with the guys tonight. I feel bad—what with Kya monopolizing my summer, and then the tumultuous and constant assessing of Ry's and my relationship—I haven't seen much of them. The plan is just to kick around my apartment and sausage-fest it, but around four or so, my phone goes off.

"Hello?" I ask, because my mother still finds caller ID disconcerting. She says whether I know or not, it's not polite to assume you know who's on the other end, and besides, she says, what if it's a police officer phoning me to tell you that your entire family has been murdered?

"It's me." It's not my mom, but it's not a police officer, either.

"Tilla? What's up?"

"You need to get me out of this house!" she exclaims, clearly infuriated. I remember how much I like not living at home.

"Why, what's going on?"

She groans. "They are driving me crazy, Niles. Legitimately crazy."

"Mom and Dad?"

"No. The Easter Bunny. Yes, Mom and Dad, Niles. Jesus!"

"Why? What are they doing?"

"Christ, I don't know? Everything? It's all, 'Matilda, have you done your homework? Matilda, have you looked into that scholarship application I emailed you? Matilda, isn't Toby Wiedermeyer such a nice boy. Does he have a girlfriend?' And guess what! I have done my homework! And I've half done that bloody application, but if they say one more word about it, I'll put it through the shredder! And Toby Wiedermeyer? Fuck! Let's just say he's not the nice little eight-year-old he used to be when he was, say, eight! In fact, he's developed into kind of an asshole! Like, totally. HELL!"

It's weird. I can totally relate. I'd just forgotten. I mean, once I moved out, my parents just started to be so happy to see me when I stopped by to do laundry, or say hello, or whatever. My dad whips me up something to eat and hands me some cash and my mom tells me they don't see enough of me and I have to come by for dinner more often. I mean, it's nice. But Matilda's explosion reminds of how tiring living at home could be. Like, always having to sneak around to have sex. It's not like my parents never said "no sex." They just sort of implied, evasively, how they did not want to hear about it or know about it, and any time Rylan and I spent alone was suspect. Having lived away from home has kind of made me forget what it is like not having sex whenever we feel like it: not having to be quiet or wait until we think everyone's asleep or whatever.

"Sorry," Matilda says, "I sound like a total sixteen-year-old, don't I? I'm just so...argh!"

"For one, I totally understand. They're parents, they get like that. And two, you are sixteen, so I think you're allowed to sound like one."

148

"And I'm a good kid! Seriously, Nigh! I've smoked like one joint, only, ever, and I don't go to a party every weekend, or bring home skeevy guys, and I haven't done anything to shatter their trust, so it's not like they have to be on my back about every little thing! And let's be honest, when Kya is my age, she is totally going to be a partier and have a new boyfriend or girlfriend or whatever probably every week and they are just going to be all, 'Oh, Kya! You are so adorable and perfect!'"

"I would say you know that's not true, except that you are probably totally right. But you're not Kya, and even though it doesn't feel like it right now, I know they think you are pretty rad in and of yourself. And if it helps, I really do understand. Rylan and I actually conducted a good portion of our relationship under that roof..."

"Good God." Matilda's voice echoes with horror. "How did you survive?"

I chuckle. "By remembering that even though they drive me crazy, I know they are just like that because they love us?"

Matilda sighs. "I know. But they still drive me friggin' nuts. Please, please, please tell me I can spend the night at your place. They can't say no to me hanging out with you. Unless you and Ry are..." She trails off.

"We're hanging out with Ian and Brice and them," I reply. "But it's cool if you want to join."

"I do. I really, really do. Thank you. Any chance you want to hit the gym for a bit first? I desperately need to run really, really fast and maybe punch something."

"Sure. See if we can borrow a car?"

"Ha. Nice try. I am so not talking to them right now."

"Oh fine, I'll ask when I get there."

"And be granted one, oh returning prodigal son. God, when can I move out?"

"In a year or so."

"Was that supposed to be comforting?"

"See you in a bit," I promise.

* * *

I feel a little guilty because Matilda is totally right: my parents seem thrilled at the idea of lending me a car. They tell me to not even worry about getting it back to them until tomorrow and that they'll carpool in the morning. They are happy to see me, and Matilda is happy to see me, and I'm guilty with luck and happiness.

Maybe that's why I have such a thing about Rylan's family, or lack of acknowledgment thereof. I mean, I can't help but think, couldn't everyone just try a little bit? He hasn't seen his mom since high school, when he moved out, and things change, don't they? All those things that used to drive me nuts in high school aren't quite as huge a deal as I thought they were. I don't know. It just feels weird to me: to have your family in the same city, and not want to see them. But I *know*, cerebrally, I mean. I know I can't push this with Rylan.

But.

Still.

* * *

Cody, my roommate, is playing COD.

"Hey, man," he says, not taking his eyes off the screen.

"Hey, bro. I'm having the guys over tonight for a bit. That all right with you?"

"Yeah, cool, sure, man." Cody, despite being somewhat unhygienic and possessing a terrifyingly limited vocabulary, is at least easygoing. "Wanna play?"

"Nah, gotta make some dinner. Thanks, though," I reply.

"I'll play," Matilda offers.

150

"Cool," Cody responds. "Wait 'til I die and I'll switch it to multiplayer."

"Awesome," I say. "Stir fry good?"

* * *

"This," Matilda announces, "is seriously addictive. How do you guys ever get anything done?"

"I don't think we do?" I'm saying, when Rylan bursts through the door.

"Get this. My boss says that if I research it and figure out how to do it right, he'll let me get a squid for one of the saltwater tanks. A squid! Seriously, how sweet is that?"

"Hey, babe." he says, kissing Matilda's head. She ignores him in favour of destroying some Nazis.

"And hey, babe," he repeats, lowering his tone to one of mock-seduction. He meets me at the doorway to the kitchen and kisses me ostentatiously.

You have to give Cody props. For someone who looks like the stereotype of a redneck-jock-homophobe, he is surprisingly blasé about the whole me and Rylan thing.

"Gonna help?" I ask, and Rylan follows me back in. He sits on the counter.

"Depends on what you mean by help...if you mean, 'provide sparkling conversation,' then yes. You bet!"

"If by, 'provide sparkling conversation,' you mean 'chop up this cucumber,' then you got it," I come back.

He hops off the counter, and leans in, lips dangerously near my ear. "When it comes to you, I've always got it," he whispers, and even if he's just playing, it still kind of turns me on.

"Jesus, Ry," I breathe.

He flashes me a devilish grin and kisses my neck before stepping back.

"So. Tell me about your day," he demands.

* * *

After dinner the rest of the guys arrive and we play this card game that Cody's Mennonite ex-girlfriend got him addicted to. Cody kicks everyone's ass, probably because he spent their eight month relationship playing it instead of getting any.

Brice's latest bedpost notch texts him repeatedly. Out loud, he bashes her, calling her clingy and annoying, but he nevertheless seems to respond to every single text she sends.

We all have a few beers and it's on about beer three that I notice that Matilda is doing that thing girls do where they touch their hair way more than necessary, and Parker's doing that thing where he keeps moving closer to my sister than is really required. I really don't know how to feel about it.

When we get sick of playing, Parker and Matilda start cleaning up. Their hands bump against each other whenever they go for same pile of cards and they keep laughing and apologizing. Rylan raises his eyebrows. Under the table his hand touches my knee, swaying it back and forth a couple of times. He's letting me make the call. If I want him to, he'll call them on it point blank, hopefully making them too embarrassed to continue this strange, fairly subtle flirtation. But if I decide I'm OK with it, then he won't say anything either.

Parker. I've known the guy for a long time. Which leads to Matilda having known the guy for a long time. He and I were in the same class in middle school. I don't remember how we became friends, but I remember we did a science fair project together. He was way more into it than I was. He goes to school with me, but is in the bio-chem department, which is almost certainly a step up from the, "I don't know what the fuck I'm doing," department in which I am enrolled.

He's a nice guy, usually pretty quiet. Hasn't had a lot of girlfriends. No serious ones, at any rate, and he's sure as hell no Brice. Regardless, I'm pretty positive three years is too much of an age gap. I mean, he's in second year and Matilda is in grade twelve. That's kind of a leap, isn't it? Of course, Matilda is probably the most mature twelfth grader you'll meet, but...would Parker really want to attend another prom? Isn't that kind of weird?

I shift my focus to Matilda. And I see her smiling. At Parker. And I'm not positive I've ever seen her smile quite like that. And then I realize: it's actually none of my fucking business. Like, even if it was Brice she was interested in—I don't have any right to interfere, or pass judgement, or whatever—I mean, she never has for me. I hear Shona in the back of mind saying something ridiculous like, "Girl's got a right to booty." I look back at Rylan and smile and shrug and he kisses me—just shy of slopping drunk.

* * *

After the game, Cody puts on some so-bad-it's-good movie that he's heard about. Parker gives me a curious cautious look before sliding in beside Matilda on the couch. I sit on the big kooshy chair in the corner and Rylan plops down on the floor in front of me, like a giant cat just begging to be stroked. He leans his head up against my legs and I appease him, toying with his hair.

We're drunk enough that the movie seems funny, but before long Cody's snoring and we're all just laughing, except Rylan, who's practically purring. Parker and Matilda are very tentatively holding hands and looking pleased. I stare at Brice incredulously, asking him if *he* sees what's going on here.

"What, man?" he whispers. "Your sister's hot shit."

I shake my head, bewildered, and stretch down, clasping my arms in front of Rylan's neck and kissing his cheek. He smiles and turns his head to kiss me properly. I really can't say I don't enjoy this newfound security. It's kind of awesome.

* * *

Eventually Cody shuffles off to bed and the rest of the guys stumble home. Matilda passes out happily on the couch.

I'm drunk and in the mood for Rylan. I push him into my room and kiss him and he kisses me. He feels so fucking good and I wanna climb him like a tree but I'm also pretty sleepy and obedient and glow under his attention as he undresses me and tucks us into bed.

"Ry?" I find myself asking.

"Yes, Drunk Niles?" he responds, pressing his lips against mine a couple more times before pulling away far enough to look me in the eyes.

"What's it like? And I'm not trying to be an asshole even if it sounds that way, but...what's it like to...not have...a family? Like, parents who are around, and sisters to look out for? I mean, you're our family now, but, you know, before?"

I lick my lips, worrying he's going to be pissed, but instead he just looks steadily at me. He slides his hand back over my side, and links my fingers with his.

"It's exactly what you'd expect," he says, calmly. "It's lonely."

"And...and you're sure that it's not in any way salvage— salva—fixable?" I question, trying, and failing, to sound sober and mature.

"Stuff between me and my parents?" he asks and I nod. "Positive. But if you really want proof, baby, I'll show you."

"It's not that I don't believe you. I just—want to know."

"Then I'll take you."

"Thanks," I whisper.

He looks at me for a long moment, then runs his hand up my arm and nips my collarbone.

"You know," he says, voice light. "I just had this wacky idea."

"Oh?" I answer, taking his bottom lip between mine for a second, "And what's that?"

He shifts closer to me, pushing his knee between mine. "What do you say to you and I having sex like normal people, just this once?"

I touch my nose to his chin, liking this idea. "And what does that involve, exactly?"

"Hmm." He considers, rolling me onto my back, only to kneel between my legs, looking down at me. "Something like this." He kisses me slowly, contently, on the mouth and neck. His hands drag up over my stomach and chest and shoulders and I grip his hair with my fingers before pulling him close.

"You know," I say. "That might just be something I could get into. But just this once."

"How opportune it is to find both of us naked, then," he whispers, lightly circling my cock with his fingers.

I gasp, smiling. "Indeed."

"Now," he instructs, "if you'd just go ahead and kiss me..."

And I do. And somewhere in the middle of it all, I swear I hear him mutter, "Kinky."

- 16 -

"Well, this is it," Rylan says, pulling my parents' car up to the curb.

We've driven for twenty minutes or so, going from the suburban neighbourhood where I grew up, through some shoddy commercial area, to here.

It's not a stereotype, exactly, like we're still in Victoria; and it's not like the front yard is filled with broken down bathtubs or old junker cars or anything. The grass is, well, not dead, but not mowed, either. The steps are cracked and the paint is peeling, and little sections of the sharply-pebbled siding have fallen or been picked off, leaving awkward bare patches. There's a not quite-rusted white Fiesta with a dark blue door in the driveway. The Venetian blinds in the biggest front window are droopy, but shut.

"She home?" I ask.

"Should be," Rylan answers, his voice flat. "Mom used to finish work around four, home by four thirty. Groceries and booze on Saturdays. So unless something's changed in the year and a bit since I last spoke to her..." He tails off, shrugging.

It still seems totally incomprehensible to me that he hasn't had contact with her for that long. Two weeks without talking to my mom, and I start to feel like a guilty little ingrate.

Rylan swings the car door shut and hits the lock button. The car honks and the lights flash. Rylan pockets the keys. He doesn't take my hand.

"Ready?" he asks, grimly.

The last time I was here was Halloween, grade ten, just a couple of months before Rylan and I started anything. None of the guys' parents (including mine) would let us crash together—it wasn't a weekend—so finally, reluctantly, Rylan said we could come over to his.

I remember he had been nervous. The house had been spotless. I realize now that that must have been Rylan's doing, but at the time I just assumed his parents were clean freaks or something. I guess I hadn't known him long enough at that point for him to divulge that his dad was rarely in the picture. I remember that Brice and Ethan were drunk, but the rest of us were sober. We'd gone trick-or-treating even though my parents had told me I was too old.

Rylan's mom didn't seem to be around, so we threw down pillows and blankets on the living room floor, eventually intending on going to bed. At some point though, Ethan, drunk out of his mind, got the genius idea of looking for the bathroom in the dark, and apparently opened the door to Rylan's mom's room instead. The rest of us were horsing around; we didn't notice he was gone.

And then we all had our first glimpse of Rylan's mom, standing in a grungy lavender bathrobe, glowering at us all.

"What the fuck is going on here, Rylan?" she'd demanded.

I'd been shocked because my parents rarely swore around us.

"Remember, Mom?" Rylan had asked, his voice unnaturally high. "I asked if I could have some guys over for Halloween? And you said it was OK?"

"Of course I remember." Her voice was sharp, biting. "But it's not Hallo-fucking-ween, yet."

Parker and I had exchanged worried glances.

Rylan bit his lip. "Yeah, Ma...it is," he said, quietly, trying to smooth over the embarrassment.

The rest of us didn't know if she was going to snap and throw something, or hit someone, or what.

Instead her expression changed completely. "Is it? Well, silly me, I didn't even carve the pumpkin." Her voice sounded as if we should all accept that this was a perfectly natural error, one that anyone would make, and that we should all just forget about it and move on. "Where is the pumpkin, baby?" She directed the question to Rylan.

"On the counter, Ma," he said, his voice wavering with helplessness. "But you bought it a couple weeks ago."

"Well? Bring it here. Me and your friends will carve it up. Isn't that right, boys?"

We hadn't known what to do, so when Rylan reappeared with a guilty, tight face, a moulding pumpkin, newspaper, and all the necessary supplies, we sat and...helped. Helped Rylan's gin-smelling mother empty out and carve a grimace into the stinking pumpkin at two a.m. on Halloween.

Rylan didn't invite us over again, after that. I'd seen his mother only twice since. Once as she walked out of a bank on a street downtown, and the other time at our high school graduation. She had to be escorted out by an administrator early, though, because she wouldn't stop cheering for Rylan. She waited for him in the lobby of the hall, where she showered him with kisses, telling him she'd started celebrating early. He'd called her a cab, and came out for dinner with my family.

I'm realizing now I really shouldn't have pushed this.

"Ry—we don't have to—"

But he just places his key in the dead bolt lock.

"Might as well," he responds. "I thought I'd keep a key so the paramedics don't have to bust down the door, when that day comes, right? But this way we can put it to use sooner."

Rylan shoves the door open. It catches on the rug inside, and he kicks that out of the way. Inside smells like I remember it: cigarettes and mould and booze, but it's not totally overwhelming. Maybe she's keeping it together well enough.

"Mom?" Rylan calls out.

There's no answer. Rylan straightens out some free city newspapers on the coffee table, and turns off the TV, which is talking to no one.

"Wait here for a sec, 'kay?" he asks me, and I nod and sit down awkwardly on the arm of the couch.

He goes upstairs and returns a minute or two later. His mom is behind him. She's dressed in slightly rumpled work clothes: a blouse and pants. Her feet are bare and her skinny arms hang uselessly to her sides, exposing big breasts and a bigger stomach, straining the blouse buttons.

"Mom, you remember Niles, right?" Rylan asks, voice soft. "My friend from school?"

"Of course," she responds impatiently, as if Rylan's re-introduction was stupid. "How are you, Myles?"

I look at Rylan for support. He crosses his arms, and I know I don't deserve a rescue. I don't bother correcting her.

"Well, thank you," I answer instead. "And yourself?"

"Oh, you know," she replies with a sigh of camaraderie. "You want something to drink? Tea or something?"

I look to Rylan, but he's still not giving me anything. "Um, sure, thanks," I say.

She claps Rylan on the back, making her way to the kitchen. "You should bring your friends round here more often, baby. Might teach you some manners, or something." It's mean. She doesn't say it in a mean way, but it's still mean.

Rylan ignores her words and my blush.

"I'll make the tea, Ma. You sit down."

159

"Don't mind if I do," she replies, and pulls out a chair, motioning for me to sit, too.

Even though Rylan hasn't lived here for years, he still seems to know his way around the kitchen, and within a few minutes the kettle is whistling, and he's pouring hot water over Red Rose tea bags in mismatched mugs. He gives a floral one to me, and a faded *Garfield* one to her. His has planets or something on it.

"How's work, Mom?" Rylan asks, carefully wrapping his fingers around the mug, and looking her straight in the eye.

"Oh, you know," she replies once again. "Rich getting richer, and all that."

"Still getting your benefits?"

"Oh yeah, they'll never take those away. I'm a good worker. Get my job done alright."

Then we surrender back into silence.

"What do you do?" I ask, finally, bravely.

"Government. Human Resources. Just make up reports, mostly. Boring shit, but someone's gotta do it, right?"

I offer a weak smile.

"What are you boys up to?" she asks, as if she'd seen us the day before and just wants to know how we spent our morning.

"Uh. I'm at school," I answer. "At the university."

She smiles. "Oh, excellent. Good for you. Beautiful campus. I used to...well. Walk around thereabouts sometimes."

"Eons ago," Rylan snorts under his breath.

His mother looks like she wants to smack him on the head, but instead she pulls her face into a smiling grimace. "Yes. Well."

There's another pause. "How come you're not getting yourself an education, Ry-baby?" she asks.

I blush. How could she say that? He managed to afford one semester before having to drop out—had to pay his rent, and

160

he refused the money my parents offered to loan him. He said there was no point paying until he knew what he actually wanted to study.

"Must be the genes," he replies.

"Don't be a shit," she fires back.

We lapse back into nothingness for another few minutes.

"So, whatcha doing down this way, anyway?" she asks.

"Just strolling through the neighbourhood," Rylan answers sarcastically. It's hard for me to watch him act this way, bitter and cold. I've never seen him like this.

"You need something?" his mom asks and I think there's genuine concern in her voice.

"Well, I did. But I suspect it's a bit too late for nourishment and sobriety."

Rylan's mother emits a pained sound, but doesn't say anything.

Ry drains his tea, and clunks his empty cup back on the table. "Look, Ma. Nigh just wanted to make sure you're doing OK. And it looks like you are. So we'll get out of your hair."

"Sure, sure." She watches him carefully until he pulls out his wallet and drops two one-hundred-dollar bills on the counter.

He looks at me. I stand and follow him towards the door. We stuff our feet back into our shoes.

"I love you, baby," we hear.

Rylan sighs and grabs my hand, suddenly and tightly, his other hand on the doorknob. "I love you, too, Mom." he says.

We leave.

* * *

For several minutes, we sit in silence. Once the car's in drive, Rylan takes my hand again, and doesn't let go.

161

Eventually we arrive at the breakwater, park, and look out over the ocean, watching seagulls dart around over the waves.

"She seems OK," I brave, finally. "Nice."

For a moment Rylan doesn't respond. When he does, it is in the form of a low, cold laugh. One I don't recognize.

"Don't," he warns. "She was totally smashed."

She was?

I don't have to say it out loud.

"Impressive, no? That's how she stays on at the office. Denial, denial, denial, and faking it."

He doesn't want me to ask, but I can't stop myself. "And you can't...do anything?"

He chuckles and then goes quiet and then chuckles again, his hand leaving mine, his eyes fixed on the side view mirror. "You're sweet, Nigh."

"Don't patronize me!" I'm frustrated and scared. I haven't seen him like this. I don't know how to react, and I just want to—I don't know, help or something.

He turns back towards me, puts his hand on my cheek, demands eye contact. "I'm not. I'm being honest. You are sweet."

"What's that supposed to mean?" I mutter, darkly.

"It means you want to find the good in people, or at least make things better, and hell, babe, sometimes you even can and that's one of the thousands of reasons I love you. But this? Nigh, you can't fix this."

"How do you know? Couldn't you...get her into a program? I mean, I know it's expensive but, maybe my parents could..."

"Your parents have thirty or forty grand kicking around?" He refutes, "Actually, even if they did, it wouldn't matter. She wouldn't take their money."

"She takes money from you," I counter.

"I'm not better than her," he replies.

"You are."

"Not to her."

I know I should shut up now but it worries at my insides and the words keep bubbling up.

"Is it—I just—Ry, I know she's fucked up. I know she hurt you, and embarrassed you and all that. But if this is going to weigh on you...I don't want you to feel—not guilty, because I don't mean guilty, but like hurt? Or remorseful?"

He shakes his head. "I can't forgive her," he says simply. "And I don't want to."

"That's a lot of anger to—"

"Look, babe, you don't understand." He smiles softly at me. "Let's walk."

I get out of the car. He walks ahead for a few paces before turning and waiting for me, taking my hand when I get close. He kisses me, and then starts walking again, quiet for a few minutes.

"There's more than I've told you about, or that you've seen," he explains, carefully. "I mean. You know I'm a sucker for my own pride, but...it can take a few hits and still survive. I've gotten over most of the shit that happened when we were kids. But—" He sighs and runs a hand through his hair. "I wasn't going to move out. You know, like I was convinced it was my duty to stay and take care of her, but, fuck—remember that night I was over at your place? And we played like, Taboo—you know, the board game? And Kya went all nutters with that annoying buzzer and chased us all around the house? And Matilda got pissed at her and you let me kiss you when I left, like a proper goodnight kiss and we'd never done that before.

"And, like, I remember being so fucking happy, when I got home, like nothing could faze me because I was with you, and your family was so good to me, and maybe I was going to be alright after all. And then of course I got home, and my mom wasn't passed out on the couch like she usually was. Instead she was sitting on the floor and she had this stupid fucking grin on her face and I knew—I just knew something was wrong."

I don't interrupt him because I don't have any words to make it better.

He keeps talking: "And she's all, 'I have a secret, baby, a surprise!' And so I said, 'Oh yeah, Mom, what's that?' And instead of answering, she just started giggling like crazy and goes, 'Look, look, look!' And so I did. And next to her week's collection of empties there's a fucking positive pregnancy test, and she goes, 'You're gonna be a big brother, baby! We're gonna be a family, finally!'"

Rylan stops and swallows. He grips my hand tight, but doesn't look at me. "It turns out she'd gotten herself knocked up at some office party, like, months earlier."

"Oh my God. Ry. I…"

He just keeps holding my hand.

"By morning, of course, she realizes she's told me and she's done a complete one-eighty, is freaking the fuck out—she can't raise another kid. The kid will be all fucked up and it will be all her fault, and kids are so much work and so much trouble and aren't even around when you need them and when can I drive her to the women's clinic so she can have an abortion? Which, fine, yeah, I want to, but she'll need to be sober for at least a few days. Which was just another layer of hell. And after that, I left. I didn't see her again until grad, where she confirmed that I had made the absolute right decision. I wasn't—I'm not going to let her drag me under. I'm worth more than that. I know it's not an easy thing to understand, especially when your family is so great, and they are, Nigh. They are so, so great, but I couldn't do it, I couldn't stay. I wanted more."

He's not crying, but I wrap my arms around him anyway, as if I am making up for all the opportunities I missed over the last few years. He clutches my sweater and bites into my shoulder and I kiss his head and stroke his back and wait.

"I'm so sorry, Ry. I'm so sorry."

His breathing sounds like it's happening for the first time ever: that the oxygen hitting his lungs is foreign and painful. There's nothing more I can say.

Except, well. "Why the fuck didn't you tell me?"

He laughs. It's sharp but honest. He kisses me hard. "I love you," he says, which does not answer the question.

"I love you, too." I reply.

"But," he starts.

"There's a but?" I demand.

He smiles and straightens the collar of my windbreaker and presses his palms flat against my chest and then kisses me again.

"Look," he says. He shakily grabs my hand and starts back towards the car, "You're...you're not the only one with completely irrational complexes."

I eye him carefully. That's news to me. "What's that supposed to mean?"

He sighs and scratches his chin. "It means—it means that I was afraid that if I showed myself, like that, to you—that you'd think I couldn't take care of you. And I can, I really, truly can, and I just...didn't ever want you to doubt me."

I shake my head in disbelief. "You're kidding me. And here all this time I was thinking that I was the fucked-up one."

He smiles bashfully. "I know, OK? I know you better than that. And I did then, too. I was just being a stupid coward."

I cannot freaking believe this. I stop walking, lean against the banister overlooking the beach, and pull him in towards me. "I really, really wish you had told me, just because I really, really wish I could have been there for you, you know?"

He looks me straight in the eyes and nods.

I keep going. "Look. I love having you, like, take care of me, or whatever. I don't know why. It's probably fucked, but I love feeling...protected, under your control, Christ, whatever the hell it is that we do, how we are. I love it. It does it for me and it's what I want, but don't you ever think, that if I had to, I couldn't take care of myself. Or that I couldn't take care of you. Because I will, any time you need it. So don't you ever fucking deny me like that again, because really you're just denying yourself, and that doesn't do anyone any good, OK?"

"Yes. OK. I got it." He nods, eyes big and deep and burrowed in mine.

"Fuck, Ry." My hands slope around the sides of his neck. "I love you so, so much. You hurt yourself alone again like that and I—I'll fucking kill you."

He smiles. "Ah, the romance that is murder threats." He kisses me and I wrap my arms around his shoulders and press my cheek against his hair and we stand like that until we start to feel OK again.

- 17 -

I meet Rylan at the bus stop downtown. He said that if it will make me feel better about how fucked up things are with his mom, he'll introduce me to his dad, because apparently their relationship is slightly less fucked up.

He looks weird. Not noticeably—he just doesn't look like himself. Like, he's wearing jeans that don't fit. Well, they fit, but not like his jeans usually fit. These are kind of baggy, he actually requires a belt. Usually he just wears a belt because they're shiny and plastic and come in fun colours or have ridiculous belt buckles, but the one he's wearing is just plain and brown. He's also wearing a T-shirt which is also not-too-big-but-bigger-than-usual and there's not another one underneath it—no layering. And it's not pink or electric blue or polka-dotted or Rylanish in any way. It's just grey. With—

"Hey! Is that my shirt?" I demand.

"Maybe." He stalls. "OK, yes. But you got it free at Orientation, so it's not like you can really claim rights to it."

Jesus. I'd pretty much forgotten about that. First year orientation: my parents made me go. Fifty bucks for the weekend; I left after a half hour. The place was swarming with lonely out-of-towners who only cared about fake IDs and the club scene. I didn't want to be the one to break it to them that so far as clubs went, they were in the wrong city.

"Fine. T-shirt rights relinquished," I allow. "But why exactly are you wearing it?"

"This is my father-friendly, dart-throwing wear," he informs me, tearing violently at a hangnail with his teeth.

167

"Really?" I state, unconvinced.

"Mmhmm." He doesn't really look at me.

"You just look—"

"Straight," he cuts me off. It's not what I was thinking but once he says it, it's obvious he's right. "I know. Promise you'll be good and play along, 'kay?" He digs around in a wallet, (a black one—one that looks nothing like the vintage *Captain Planet* zip-pouch he usually pockets) for his bus pass.

"Crap, Ry, you should have said something, I mean...I didn't think..."

"You always look straight," he says, flatly, eyes scanning the upcoming buses for our number. It pulls up and he steps on. He takes the window seat, which is unusual. He tends to prefer boxing me in.

I don't drop it.

"What does that mean, even?"

"You know." He sighs. "People assume you're straight. People aren't quite sure what to assume about me."

He slings his arm up onto the window ledge, with none of his usual poise. Instead his movements are sullen and deliberate and strangely masculine, not that I've ever thought of him as not masculine. It's just...this is different. It's like suddenly he should be out drinking beers and talking about cars. Except that's not right, because he does those things, we both do. You can't grow up friends with Brice and not end up knowing more than you ever wanted to about V8 engines and torque. I just find it kind of disconcerting to see Rylan looking so unnatural in his skin.

I don't push it though, just shrug and give him a you-win face and go to kiss him.

He lets me but then says, "No more, OK? We're just bros, today, alright? I know it sucks but I have to compartmentalize. You and my dad in the same room. Jesus, this will be weird."

168

I remove my hand from the collar of his-slash-my T-shirt, and he doesn't reach for me. "Yeah, alright. Sorry," I say.

"No, I'm sorry. I just—give it a few years. You'll get used it." He offers me a defeated little smile and I feel guilty or something. Rylan's been living this private life that I don't even know about, while he knows my life inside-out and backwards. I can't tell if I'm feeling cheated out of something or protected, but either way I wish I wasn't so in the dark. It makes him and me on uneven footing. Or else it just makes me a jerk for never asking the right questions, or him a jerk for hiding all the answers.

"So. Should you quiz me on sports stats or some other manly topic? What do you and your dad talk about, even?" I ask, lamely. Sitting this close to him without him touching me is unsettling. My gut instantly suspects that things are wrong between us, even if cerebrally I know they aren't.

"We don't. We just drink beer and throw darts. It's easy. You'll be fine," he affirms.

"That or I'll fuck it up."

"Well. Don't," he replies, not very helpfully.

"Thanks for that."

He offers me a token grin and I guess I feel a little more at ease, but not much.

"You know, you're lucky this bus is full, or you sitting here would be totally gay," he informs me.

"What?"

"Bro code. You never sit next to your bro if there are seats available across the aisle or behind, or in front. It is decidedly gay to sit next to your bro."

"Uh. OK." Not really something I'd thought about. "You a strict observer of bro culture?"

"Are you kidding? Watch Brice next time. He can't bring himself to sit next to any of us. Across the aisle, behind, in

169

front, but never beside. He'll take up two seats if he possibly can. I mean, I love Brice like a brother, but he is a total bro and, to be frank, kind of a shit."

He's right. About Brice anyway.

"I'm sure I've sat next to Parker," I counter.

"Parker's hardly a bro," Rylan retorts.

I raise an eyebrow. "Yeah, but he's straight."

"Yeah. But doesn't feel the need to prove he's straight. Brice does."

"You've certainly put a lot of thought into this," I observe.

"Either I assimilate or I don't see my dad at all. I can only handle being estranged from so many parents at once, you know?"

Christ, I cannot fuck this up on him. "Should I have some kind of a training manual or something?"

He laugh and shakes his head. "No. Don't worry, Alberta. You look straight and he thinks I'm straight, so the thought won't even cross his mind. You're just a buddy of mine who likes beer and darts. No problems."

At least I like beer.

* * *

I make it through the first pitcher and the first game.

Rylan wasn't lying when he said his father didn't talk much. He mostly just listened as Rylan described the renovation being done to the back room at his work. I barely knew the reno was occurring, let alone details about the uneven drywalling and the resulting kerfuffle between Rylan's boss and the construction foreman. I mean, I'm not exactly surprised he hasn't told me, because I've since realized that I don't actually give a shit about home renos, or, in this case, work renos. I've always just assumed that Rylan feels the same way, but it actually sounded like he knew what he was talking about. His dad, Darrell, sat there, jean-jacketed, tan-faced and horseshoe-mustached, just nodding along, like he knew what the fuck Rylan was saying, and asking questions about routing pipes or something. Questions that Rylan seemed to have legitimate answers to.

Rylan didn't look at me. He certainly didn't touch me. There were no quick glances to check on me and no hand grazing my knee under the table. There were no affectionate or sarcastic pet names and worst of all there was no sense that Rylan—the Rylan I know—was even there at all.

I realized that this is what it must be like for him: that to maintain the last familial relationship he has, he has to pretend he's not himself. That knowledge—it just freaked me out. I felt claustrophobic and overheated and scared and so I just—left. I drained my glass, and said I needed a smoke, and that they could get started on the next round without me and then I left.

I knew Rylan wouldn't contradict me in front of his smoker father, and besides, I wasn't lying. Fuck was I ever not lying. I practically ran across the street to buy a pack of du Mauriers and a lighter at a gas station and once I had them I just sank on the curb, lit and inhaled.

I haven't smoked in over two years and for the life of me I don't know how Ry ever convinced me to give them up. This is what I need. When things in my head get messy, these are what calm me down.

These, and him. Fuck.

* * *

"You know I hate when you do that."

Rylan's voice beside me makes me jump. I didn't expect him to follow me, but now that he's here I realize I should have

171

known better. I needlessly complicate shit and he resolves it and that is how we work.

I take one long, last drag before stubbing the thing out and dropping it next to the previous two butts, just because he told me to, or because he was going to tell me to. I do it just because the only thing that settles me better than tobacco is his voice relieving me of the responsibility of decision-making.

The last thing I want is what I suspect is coming. He's never given one before, but maybe I've never deserved it before: a lecture on my own immaturity and histrionics and if he thinks I don't know that I'm acting like a child he's beyond wrong. However, just because I know I'm doing it doesn't mean I know how to stop. I'm panicked. I can't go back into that bar, that alternate universe, where Rylan isn't gay and doesn't touch me and cares about shit I know nothing about.

I can feel his eyes on me but I can't look. This isn't like me. We both know that. I don't run: I ignore and persevere. My fingers go searching for another cigarette.

"Niles."

I drop the pack and flick the lighter instead, saying nothing.

"I can't fix it if you don't tell me what's wrong."

He's using his voice—the voice. The one he uses when he's about to fuck me, the one that simultaneously increases my heart rate and soothes my nerves, makes me absolutely certain he wants me, at least for the upcoming moments.

I try to maintain some semblance of control in my voice when I say, "If I stay in there any longer, I'll fuck it up."

"What do you mean?" Does he have to be so goddamn patient? Could he maybe get mad? Give me some justification to ditch the entire situation?

"I can't do it."

"Do what? We're not doing anything. You're doing fine. He doesn't suspect a thing."

172

"Good. Great." I don't even try to make it sound like I mean it.

"Do you—do you want me to come out to him? I'll do a lot of things for you, Nigh, but that kind of crosses a line." There's an angry bite to his tone that I've rarely heard before.

"No," I counter, immediately—and I don't. I can tell just from meeting the guy that that would mean the end. It's a pitiful relationship, but it's all Rylan has. I have no right whatsoever to want him to give that up.

"Then what?" He still hasn't touched me and I'm going mostly crazy. For fuck's sake; for the last three years, even when I convinced myself, and half-convinced Shona, that whatever Rylan and I had was over, that I was crazy, that we were just friends, or that he didn't even slightly love me, it just took one touch from him, one possessive arm around my shoulders or hint of teeth on my earlobe to re-install hope, or relief or certainty.

So this, this is...

"You," I gasp it out. "You can't condition me to need something and then just cut me off, cold turkey. No warning."

"What? Babe, what are you talking about?" He tries to interject, but I barely hear him. The floodgates are up and I can't stop myself.

"And since when do you care about goddamn renos? You at least could have told me. I would have listened."

"You hate that shit," he replies, stunned. "My dad used to work construction, he's into that sort of thing. But whatever, that doesn't matter. What do you mean, condition you?"

"Like...God. This is beyond insane. Something's wrong with me. I'm going home. Tell your dad I said thanks for the beer."

I grab the pack of smokes before standing on unreasonably wobbly legs. I try not to look at Rylan but I catch his surprised

173

expression in the gas station window anyway. I hate it, seeing him not knowing what to do.

* * *

Of course, I only make it about two steps before his hand clutches my wrist and bungees me back towards him.

"Oh, fuck no," he says. "You at least have to let me know things are all right with us. Christ, just what are you walking away from even?"

His fingers automatically find mine and relief plummets through me. The concern in his eyes and the confusion in his voice is disarming and painful and everything I was feeling seems shoddy and weak in comparison.

"I'm sorry," I say, stupidly, regretfully, ashamedly. I step in closer and he doesn't back away. I register that I'm more important than spectators. I knew that, of course. I know that, but panic is hard to reason with.

"OK," he says. "Can you tell me what's going on?"

"I guess...I guess I had expectations of how this would go. And it didn't go that way, and so that threw me off, and when I get thrown off I usually just go to you to make it better, but I couldn't, because you were right in the middle of it and..."

"You're not making a ton of sense here, babe," he says, hands sympathetic on my shoulders.

"Ugh. Uh. Fuck." I shake my head with useless frustration.

"Words? Please?" he prompts, gently.

I bite my lip but then spit it out. "Look, Ry, I don't think I understood just how much of a charade you put on for your father's benefit. I feel like I was totally blindsided by this and I tried to let you know but you weren't talking to me or looking at me or touching me and, like, all my pathetic insecurities came slamming back into me and you, the you I know, wasn't even there and Christ! Since tenth frickin' grade, any time I have been around you, you have found excuses to, like, put your hands on me. And we didn't talk about what was going on for so long, that I guess I kind of substituted that for verbal reassurance. So when you take that away from me, without warning, I just get crazy or something and panic. I don't know. It's weird and it freaked me out and I didn't know what to do, so I had to get out of there."

He looks kind of bewildered. "But it's not like I'm touching you every second of every day. I mean, I go to work. You go to school. We do all right doing our own thing. I don't know why this would be different."

"No, no. When you're not around, it's not a problem because I know you're not touching me because you're not around. When you are around...fuck, you are always all over me. Like, before we even got together you used to fuck around in French class, kicking me and writing on my arm, and you always made a point of being near me—you always chose me and never the other guys and it just felt really good and I didn't know I'd come to depend on it and to expect it, but I guess I know now."

Rylan gapes kind of hopelessly at me. "I guess. I never really thought...I mean. Yeah. You're right. And it's not like it didn't mean anything, but...I just like touching you. I didn't mean it to be..."

"This big thing," I fill in. "I know. But somehow I interpreted it as that, and it's kind of just stuck. So I'm gonna go. Because you're too good at pretending, and I'm a little too messed up to know better, and now I'm feeling really fucking embarrassed and more than a little stupid, so I'm...Yeah. Gonna go."

"OK." He doesn't sound convinced. "You need anything? Like, should I...?" He trails off, miserably.

"No," I resolve. "No. I'm good. Humiliated, but fine. You go."

He gives me a quick, tight hug, one arm hooked roughly around my neck, and he kisses me on the ear. "If it makes you feel better, I really fucking *wanted* to touch you."

"OK, yeah. It kind of does."

"I'll call you later, yeah?"

"That would be good. I promise not to count down the minutes or wait by the phone. I'll...go out and be independent or something."

"Yeah, good plan. Sounds like you might need it," he suggests.

"Fuck you," I reply, without venom.

He grins. "Talk to you tonight."

* * *

On the bus ride home I decide that talking shit out isn't quite as terrifying as I somehow convince myself it will be.

I should try to remember that more often.

- 18 -

come over

Rylan doesn't text often, so I'm a little surprised when I check my phone.

"Anything good?" Shona asks. I've been recounting the meeting-the-parents debacle of the previous week while we sip iced coffee.

"Just Rylan," I shrug, and quickly fire off a text:

With Shona. Catch you later.

Shona takes a long swig of her coffee then her eyes go wide and she grips her forehead. "Fuck. Brain freeze."

I grimace in sympathy. My phone goes off again.

maybe you didn't understand. when i said come over i meant now

My cheeks flush with heat and Shona takes a break from her self-pitying to snatch my phone out of my hand.

"Christ on a cracker," she whistles. "Controlling much?"

"Uh…" I mumble.

Shona rolls her eyes and laughs. "Well, I can't compete with that." My phone buzzes in her hand and she reads: "'dont fucking keep me waiting.'" She shakes her head. "Seriously, Nigh? Like, look me in the eye and tell me you honestly enjoy this sort of thing."

The last thing I want to do is look anyone in the eyes. I feel hot and uncomfortable and all I want is to go over and be with him, be good for him.

I also know that I won't be able to enjoy it if I'm feeling guilty about making Shona guilty. So I lift my chin, and I catch her eyes and I shrug. "I do. When it's him, I do."

Her lips twist in doubt. "You promise?" she insists.

"Yeah. I do, but if I ever don't, you're my go-to girl, OK?"

"I'd better be." She gives me a half-smile. "Also, can't your man find the apostrophe key?"

"I guess punctuation isn't what's on his mind right now."

Shona rolls her eyes. "Get out of here."

"Thanks." I kiss her offered cheek. "Love you. Call you soon."

"Yeah, yeah." But she grins as she rolls her eyes again and I know I don't have to feel bad about ditching her.

* * *

The bus ride, as predicted, is hell. I'm anxious with anticipation and horny as fuck. It takes fifteen minutes just for the fucking thing to arrive (late), and then when it finally does arrive, we're held up by a woman who can't seem to figure out how to steer her motorized scooter on and off the bus. But finally, *finally*, the bus lurches forward—and my stomach flutters in sympathy.

* * *

I knock and Ry doesn't answer, so I try the door handle. It's unlocked. Taking a deep breath, which does absolutely nothing to calm the hailstorm in my chest, I open it and enter.

From the front door I can see him, sitting on the couch in the living room. The lights are all on, and even before he says anything, I feel pathetically exposed.

His posture is lazy, but his eyes sharp.

"Strip," he demands.

I don't hesitate, dumbfounded by his ever-constant ability to reduce me to this flustered, wanting mass of matter. By the time my jittery fingers pull away my shirt and shorts and boxers, my dick is rock hard and prominent, begging for attention—his attention.

"Come here," he directs.

I take a shaky step forward.

"Uh uh uh," he scolds, voice quiet in its teasing, but dangerous. "On your knees."

This is absurd. A main part of me knows, *knows*, that I should be feeling utterly ridiculous right about now. It's the only rational response to this situation, but Rylan and I, we've never been rational. So, I don't. Instead I feel entranced, trapped, controlled. I drop to my hands and knees without question and approach him, crawling carefully between the couch and the footstool, stopping and kneeling at his feet.

"Good boy," he says, an unconcerned palm dropping heavily on my head, stroking my hair.

Fuck. I could bask in his attention for every second of every day of the rest of my life and never need a single other goddamn thing in the entire world.

His hand stills and I look up at him, "Now what?" written clearly on my face. He stretches one hand over the back of the couch, relaxes the other onto to the arm rest.

"What the hell do you think?" he responds, sinking back into the cushions, legs parted obviously.

179

My fingers, trembling with something, I'm not sure what—desire or anxiety, or more likely a mixture of both—reach for his fly, detouring over his thighs.

"That's enough with your hands, I should think." Rylan's voice, infiltrated with dominant arrogance, stops my motion before I undo the top button. For a moment I miss his meaning, and glance up at his face for clarification. His tongue darts menacingly out of his mouth, then hooks a retreat, and I get it. Resting my hands on his upper thighs, I press my face into his clothed crotch, feeling his erection against my cheek and nose. He sighs appreciatively and shifts forward slightly into the pressure and I want him. I want to feel his cock against my skin, in my mouth.

I tackle the top button and discover that this is a lot fucking harder than I expected. I have to bite down on the felt-ish material at the waistband of his pants, pull that taut, and then manoeuvre the button through the slot with my tongue. Thank fuck he's not wearing jeans or something. It takes me a while, and I keep expecting Rylan to get impatient and just do it for me, which terrifies me because I can't disappoint him, not again, all I ever do is disappoint him when I want so much to be good. Determinedly I finally align the button in just the right way and shove it through, glancing up at him victoriously once I've succeeded. His expression is one of languid amusement, and that sends a streak of exhilarated shame through me. I'm a game, a pet, a dependant.

And maybe if I behave, he'll fuck me.

I take his zipper in my teeth and draw it down. His cock springs free, almost smacking me in the face and he chuckles. I stare at it for a moment. Rylan's cock. Truthfully, I think it's more familiar than my own. There's a hint of pre-cum at the tip and I'm swamped with an ecstatic sense of pride. I did that.

"Kiss it," he orders.

I do, immediately, and without question, half ignoring and half revelling in the small strings of jizz that attach themselves to my lips, making me feel cheap and filthy and aching.

Rylan doesn't need to tell me what to do next. I'm absolutely resolute on bestowing upon him the best blow job ever recorded in human history. After bathing his cock from every angle I can get at from my position at his feet, I suck him off, swallowing him whole and constricting my throat around him, allowing peristalsis to massage his prick, simultaneously trying my best to keep from audibly gagging. Hands providing leverage, I thrust my face as close into his body as I possibly can: holding and swallowing and holding and swallowing until I swear I'm going to pass out, and then releasing and diving back on. Saliva and pre-cum spill out over my chin, and I know I must look like a sloppy whore, but I don't care. I'm getting what I want: Rylan's groans are sounding in the back of his throat, and he's growling at me, "Fuck, baby," and, "That's my dirty boy," and, "You were made for sucking cock—a natural born cocksucker, aren't you?" and he's never called me that before, but somehow I like it, have craved it, even, without ever knowing. His hands grip my hair, and I almost regret requesting a break from the breath play because suddenly I want it. Wish he would hold me like this until I went under, and then wish he'd fuck my throat hoarse and my ass raw, me unconscious all the while. The thought makes me whine with need, desperate to be used in any way he sees fit.

He promised no choking though, and so he rips my mouth off of him, fist in my hair, catching me off-guard. Forcefully, he swivels and flings me forward over the ottoman. He catches my flailing arms and pins them to my back under his bony, threatening knee, and commences a vicious attack on my ass. Harsh, unveiled smacks are unleashed upon my naked skin. I can't help myself. I cry out, unable to hold back as he hits me hard and fast, railing on the same spot several times before moving on, and then returning. My dick is trapped between my body and the scratchy fabric of the ottoman, but that doesn't seem to subdue my raging hard-on. In fact, I find myself rutting unevenly against the furniture as Rylan's punishment painfully continues.

"You dirty bitch." His voice is incredulous and mocking. "You like this, don't you?"

I grunt a nonsensical reply and thrust my ass upwards to receive the next round of blows. I'm not disappointed. He's kneeling half on me and uses the leverage to his advantage: he does not hold back. "Answer me!" he demands.

"Yes. Yes, sir," I whisper between gritted teeth. Of course I like it. He wouldn't be doing it if I didn't like it.

The assault ceases. He strokes my tender and inflamed ass with a graceful palm. "Sir. I like that," he considers, softly. "Spread your legs."

I do, until I'm poised on the balls of my feet, teetering awkwardly, with my torso pressed into the ottoman. He gives my inner thighs a couple of well-placed whacks, and squeezes my balls cruelly, reducing me to a desperation-spurred near-keening. Nevertheless, my erection flags: his obvious desired effect. For a moment there's nothing, just waiting—terrible, traumatizing, waiting. Gently, he releases my hands from beneath his knee and gathers my wrists behind my head. The silky-smooth fabric of some kind of binding tightens around them. I should have known.

He kisses my shoulder blade and gives my ass one firm and final, loving swat, causing me to yelp miserably.

"Well, darling, let's get you to bed," he proposes. His voice is sweet and incongruous. I feel his eyes scour me. "Or maybe not quite just yet," he remedies. "Turn over."

I do so, clumsily rolling onto my back, still arched uncomfortably over the footstool. He casually straddles me, his cock bouncing in my face. He balances one knee on the ottoman beside me, before hooking a sure hand in my hair and dragging my face up towards his dick. A few choking stabs into the back of my throat, the zipper of those fucking pants he's still wearing burning strips against my neck, and he's coming messily, half in my mouth and half on my face. He drops my head and gives a satisfied groan, sitting unceremoniously upon my stomach.

With his eyes half-closed, he traces curlicues onto my chest with his fingertips, recuperating. I try surreptitiously to keep the sticky saliva/cum compound on my face from entering my nose and eyes, only semi-successfully. The delicious humiliation of it all causes my cock to regain hardness and I writhe beneath him, knowing he won't give me any relief—not yet.

It only takes Rylan a couple of minutes to regain himself. He smiles wolfishly at me before running his hands over my triceps and forearms to take my hands in his, face inches away from mine.

His tongue emerges and he licks a stripe of slime off my chin before kissing me, passing the mixture from his mouth to mine, and then touching his lips to my throat to insist that I swallow.

"Open your mouth," he instructs, and then he finishes sponging up my face with his tongue, licking up the remnants of his cum and then dripping it, now combined with his saliva, into my waiting mouth from varying heights. I feel cored: exhaustively and totally owned. The procedure seems highly entertaining to Rylan, however, and he goes about the task with a certain obscene diligence. When he considers the job done, he kisses me again in earnest. My balls ache and I don't know how much longer I can wait.

He fists my bound wrists and manoeuvres me into standing, marching me in the direction of his bedroom. I can probably count the number of times we've actually had sex in his bed on one hand. We still don't come here much.

I stumble a couple of times on the way over, but he doesn't let me fall. "Knees," he commands, motioning to the bed. I obey and watch as Rylan attaches the binding around my wrists to a pre-set binding on the headboard slats, a couple of feet from the mattress. Knowing that he consciously planned this for me, for us, sends a brilliant thrill through my guts. Displacing the pillows, he directs my head downwards, straining my arm sockets uncomfortably. He runs a hand over my vertebrae and kisses my lower back, patting my still-hot, still-sore, ass.

He stands and strips and takes his cock in his hand, scrutinizing my body as he slowly strokes himself hard. I groan out of either pain or want, I'm not sure, but my thighs part for him as he positions himself behind me and reaches for my cock for the first time since the proceedings began. He jacks me conscientiously for maybe a minute, before pausing to lube up his fingers and my ass. The cool solution contrasts addictively with the heat radiating from the thrashing I received—and that's when it all kind of clicks. This is going to hurt like a son of a bitch.

He slaps my ass hard. Foreshadowing. "You want me to fuck you?" he demands, but there's no real urgency in his voice. His fingers probe roughly at my asshole and he knows the answer.

"Fuck. Yes."

He smacks me again. "Manners, Alberta."

I grit my teeth, keeping myself from coming just yet, as he toys once more with my dick. The fingers in my asshole light over my prostate and I find myself gasping and squealing.

"Please, Rylan. Please fuck me, please. I'll be so good for you, I'll make you feel so good. Please just fuck me." He makes a satisfied sound and holds me open and I realize that's the first time I've said his name during sex.

He doesn't ease into things, instead shoving inside me with less-than-optimal preparation, but that's not the primary source of pain. No, it's the smashing of his pelvis into my abused ass cheeks that really fucking kills. The rough hairs on his thighs irritate the tortured skin, adding to the burn, and his balls slap against me in what seems like a calculated attempt at degradation. With one hand, he forces my neck down, grinding my forehead and nose into the sheets, wrenching my shoulders in their sockets. He utilizes his newfound leverage to fuck me even deeper. The hackneyed fingernails of his free hand gouge into me. They scrape relentlessly over my inflamed flesh until I'm positive the skin will give way to blood, if it hasn't already.

I thrust my ass towards him, urging him to go faster, to fuck me to completion, but instead he slaps my ass, reminding me, in case I miraculously forgot, just who is in charge here. Urgent noises escape out of my throat, and he staggers his thrusts maddeningly. Suddenly he pulls out of me fully, and slaps at my flank until I realize what he wants. I roll gracelessly over, my fresh-made wounds scraping against the duvet. He hikes my knees up to my aching shoulders, lines his cock head up with my hole and then drives into me. My cock leaks between our bodies and Rylan leans in and presses his mouth against mine, hungrily.

Every instance of pain that sparks inside of me hitches me closer and closer towards coming. He pulls back and his eyes catch mine for a moment before he sinks his teeth into my chest, angling his cock just so.

"Three," he says, and there's a smudge of blood on his lips from where he bit me. I can barely feel it, my ass is so on fire. His hips slam against me, and I scream as his dick glances over my prostate.

"Two." He kisses me and I swear I can taste his cum, our saliva, my blood, separate entities combined between us. He pounds into me again, and my brain can't decide which it wants to register more: my tortured ass cheeks or my rejoicing prostate.

His nose streaks a path to my ear, which he nips, then kisses. His hand wraps possessively around my cock, and he fucks me brutally, perfectly, beautifully, and he whispers, "And come."

* * *

In my daze of afterglow, I barely register him continuing, fucking my pain-wracked, satisfied body. I only remember the moment of his completion and collapse: cum, sweat, spit, blood on the bed sheets, and I don't care. This power, this intensity, this enormity: this is how I want to be wanted.

- 19 -

I'm a wreck when Rylan wakes me up. He's showered and half-dressed, jeans that are more holes than denim ride low on his hips.

My ass is beyond killing me; it is throbbing with a perpetual, deep-reaching ache. My wrists are still tied behind my neck. My shoulders hate me as I slide up onto my lower back, pulling at my already exerted joints. There's blood drying on my chest from where he bit me. It doesn't look deep but it stings and is ragged and messy as hell.

"How you doing?" Rylan asks, a light smile playing on his lips. He reaches out and brushes a gentle hand over my cheek, and the gentleness of it does things to me. He stuffs some pillows between my back and the headboard, relieving some of the pressure on my shoulders, but my wrists still pulsate with displeasure.

He's got a damp cloth that he's using to dab at my various sex wounds. It's obviously saturated with some kind of medical agent, because it stings like a bitch. I secretly love him when he's like this, all nurturing and conscientious.

"Thanks," I mumble, thickly. "You gonna untie me?"

He ignores me until he's wiped up all the blood and cleaned out the bite marks.

"Not just yet," he establishes.

"Rylan. My arms are fucking falling off."

"I know. I'm sorry. Here." He loosens the knot a little bit. Blood trickles back into my hands. The pins and needles are nauseating. "Roll over for a sec, baby boy. I'll take care of your back."

Willingly, I struggle onto my side, exposing my back to him. He applies the antiseptic or whatever to the eight or nine long scratches he bore into the skin on either side of my spine. The sting is brutal, but it fades quickly. His palm grazes my ass curiously and I can't stop myself from hissing sharply.

He lets out a low whistle. "Shit," he observes. "I look good on you." Gently, he helps me roll back over, easing one arm under my neck and shoulders. "You think I took it a little overboard?" He slips his hand out from underneath me to cautiously touch my face.

"If by overboard you mean the hottest sex we've ever had?" I say, feeling a lightheaded goofiness temporarily fill me.

"I was hoping you would say that," he replies, leaning in and taking my bottom lip between his and sucking on it gently. I kiss him back and he puts a hand in my hair and I want to just wrap an arm around his neck and lie half on top of him and go back to sleep. "Oh," he whispers, dropping kisses all over my face, "just for the record, you're not a slut. Or a bitch. Or a cocksucker. Or anything I may or may not remember calling you prior to or during fucking. Just in case you were on the verge of obsessing."

"Fuck off," I answer him, although given my history he makes a good point.

"I just wanted to make sure you knew."

"Well, thanks for the concern. But I sort of *am* a cocksucker. In case you haven't noticed."

"Oh, I've noticed." He presses his face into my chest and groans. "But you don't possess any of the negative connotations."

188

I roll my eyes and he kisses my neck. "You're ridiculous. Seriously, though, untie me, would you? There's no way I can handle another round right now."

He pulls back until he's sitting next to me. His face looks kind of pale and he's suddenly nervous as hell. "Um," he says, "I can't do that."

"What do you mean? Use scissors or something."

"No, that's not what I mean. I mean, I can undo it, but. I need to talk to you about something first, and I need you to hear me out. So I can't untie you, because you'll try to run and I need you to stay here."

* * *

If time could freeze, it just did.

There's an intense sinking feeling in my gut and I want to run already—run or throw up, or even tell him to maybe just not say anything instead, because maybe ignorance really is bliss. This absolutely cannot be any good. My imagination goes fucking insane with ideas. He's going to...move away, or else he wants to see other people, or else he doesn't want me, after all, or worse? He wants me to fuck someone else for his benefit, which I absolutely will not do, even if it means I'm tied up here forever. He thinks it's better if we break up. He's met someone else. He's not gay after all. He can't keep hiding his sexuality from his father. He's chosen his dad over me. No, I try to calm myself, we just had sex. It can't be that, unless, Jesus fuck, was that goodbye sex? Oh my fucking God, no. I'm going to hyperventilate.

I steel myself as best I can, which isn't very well, and finally, just ask, "What exactly do you need to talk about?"

He bites his lip and stares me in the eye, his hand on my face, thumb stroking my cheekbone softly and I want to shake him off if he's going to hurt me, but I want him to keep doing it if this is the last time.

"Look. I'm not lying when I say you need to hear me out. So please don't say anything until I get it out. Just listen, all right?"

"I'm not making any promises." My voice is cold, accusatory.

"Please, baby?" he begs, gently.

"Just talk," I hiss, though I'm probably lying.

"OK," he says. "Fuck. OK. Here goes."

I stare him down, trying to make him feel just as shitty as I do in this moment.

"Look, Niles." He exhales softly, and sweeps some hair off my forehead. "You know I love you." This cannot be good. Anything that starts with, "You know I love you," by universal law or something must follow with a cruel, horrible, "but…"

But it doesn't. He just keeps talking. "And you know I'm crazy about your family. And…I've talked to your parents, and they've agreed to lend me the money so that I can go back to school."

This is so far off from where I thought it was going that I don't even know how to react, but he just continues, "I know I should have mentioned it before, but I didn't want to say anything until it was for sure and I didn't want you to feel awkward and have to choose sides between me and your parents. I mean, money gets between people, and you would get weird about it. You know you would."

I sputter, but he's probably right. I'd try to convince my parents that it was a good idea, and if they weren't for it, it would be awkward as fuck, but I guess they were, so…But this means—this means what, exactly? Like, he's going back to school, so what? Rylan's words aren't stringing together any semblance of sense.

"So—you're moving or something?" I ask, utterly unable to keep quiet, or my voice steady.

He raises his eyebrows, a confused expression on his face.

"What? No! I need to do upgrading at the college first, but then there's a program here—nursing—I didn't say. I think I wanna be a peds nurse, because of all the stuff with Kya and visiting her there and it just seemed—but Jesus, I'm rambling, we can talk about that later. That's not what I want to talk about. I just wanted to show you before I talk to you about what I *do* want to talk about that I, you know, have a plan. I know you think I'm just kind of wandering around aimlessly half the time."

He's a bit right. I mean it doesn't bother me that he doesn't have his life all mapped out, I mean, who does?

"But I swear I'm not. I've put a lot of thought into it and I really want to hang out with kids and also do some good, and it means I can get work pretty much anywhere, hopefully, so you can do your thing if you want to and—again we really don't need to go into all that right now."

I seriously had no idea Rylan ever thought about the future, like, at all, so I kind of just stare at him. Finally, I swallow and say, "OK. So. That's good. I mean. I'm happy for you, Ry, but that's not the kind of thing that is going to make me run away, so would you please just tell me what exactly is going on?"

He bites his lip and taps his fingertips anxiously against my ribs. "Christ." He exhales, then looks me straight in the eyes. "Niles, I want you to marry me."

* * *

I don't know if it's a minute or a second or an hour that I sprawl there, tied up and bug-eyed and utterly unable to form anything resembling human speech.

"What?" I finally spew out. Ineloquent as fuck, but what the hell else am I supposed to say?

"Please don't talk." He presses his fingers to my lips. "I know. You're freaking out. Don't freak out. Just listen."

I shake my head free. This is not happening. He's lost it. What's wrong with him? We're not even twenty-one.

"Untie me."

"No."

"Rylan. Untie me."

"No. I will. I mean if you really want me to, I will, but you said you'd try. Please just hear me out. And then I'll untie you. I promise. So will you stay? Just like this? Just for a minute?"

"Fine." I grit my teeth. The bastard certainly knew what he was doing. Of course I would try to run. He's being completely irrational. He might be totally brainless, but I'm not. People our age are not supposed to get married. They just mess everything up. They ruin the relationship and bicker all the time and make everyone around them uncomfortable. Plus they are a total financial drain on their families. How many times have I seen people roll their eyes when they hear about two stupid kids getting hitched? How many sarcastic comments and predictions of failure? Why would he want that for us? Things are good, great—fuck, we've only just learned to talk shit out. Why the hell is he doing this?

"It makes sense."

He goes to caress my face, but I jerk away from him, so he opts for resting his hand on my chest instead.

"If you think I don't know what you're thinking, you're wrong. You're thinking this is ridiculous, that I'm insane, but I'm not. Think about it. We've been together for almost four years."

Three and a half, I correct him in my head.

"And you know I'm completely crazy about you."

192

Or just crazy, I add, silently.

"And I don't want to be with anyone else. And you don't either."

So what? Just because we don't want to be with anyone else doesn't mean we should get frickin' *married*. What is *wrong* with him? I go to talk but he cuts me off.

"Niles, I've been lonely my entire life."

There's a deep, hollow sadness in his voice that I hate, because Rylan's loneliness is something I've worked hard at denying, along with his other weaknesses, for years.

"And then I met you. And from then on, it didn't matter what my fuck-up of a family did, because I had a new one, a better one, but mostly, I had you." He gives me a nervous little smile. "Which means, you're pretty much all I've thought about for the last four years."

He looks at me, waiting. The words are intense, of course they are, but Christ. What have I been doing with my life since I met him? Obsessing, constantly, over him. It's practically all I do. And when I haven't been obsessing over him, it's because I've been with him, or because he's been there to help me handle everything else I might need to obsess about—Kya and school and Tilla's newfound dating habits...

But still. That doesn't mean we should get married. I mean, come on!

"And I'm not saying I want to get married tomorrow. I'm thinking in like a year or six months or something. I've saved up some money." He rattles on. "Well, not, like, a fortune. But I've been working at Nook since I was fifteen, and I've saved the better part of it. I take care of myself. You know I do, and you know I can take care of you—that I will take care of you." He's got his hand along my jaw and veracity in his eyes.

And for some stupid reason, part of me starts to want it. But. Really? Like...really? Marriage?

"We're too young," I mutter.

"No, we're not. We're young, sure. But lots of, like, religious couples get married way younger than us. Hell, people we graduated with are already celebrating anniversaries."

"Christian kids get married so they can have sex. We're already having sex," I point out.

"Don't be so cynical!" Rylan argues. "Maybe they get married because when they realize they're in love, that's it. They can stop looking. Besides, your parents weren't much older than us when they got married, and it worked out for them. Not everyone who gets married young is religious."

"Then it's because they're pregnant. Again, not something we really need to worry about."

"So what are you saying?" he challenges. "That we're not really in love because we're not old enough? That we can't get married because we don't believe in God, or because we're not about to have a kid?"

"No. You know that's not what I think. It's just. There's...stuff. Things I want to do..." I don't know how to finish my sentence and I wish my hands weren't fucking tied above my head, so that I could at least cover my face and surrender. I tug sharply at the restraints, but the knots don't loosen. Rylan rubs my wrists meaningfully.

"I know," he soothes. "I know that, but babe, I'm not asking you to take out a mortgage and adopt a Chinese baby and file for life insurance. I just want you to be with me. And, anyway, all that stuff you want to do, like graduating and travelling and, I don't know, finding a career—do you really picture doing all that on your own?"

I... No. Of course I don't. Every time I picture myself taking off to explore Norway or Vietnam or wherever I happen to think I might want to go someday, Rylan is always there with me. When I think about Kya's birthdays, or Matilda's prom, I can just see Rylan there, dressed preposterously for the occasion and passing out forks, because it would be weird, off, terrible, if he wasn't there, because he's already a permanent fixture in my life.

But even still, marriage is...big.

"Couldn't we just...move in together?" I ask.

He fiddles with his tongue piercing between his teeth. Shakes his head. "No."

I wait for him to elaborate.

"I know this sounds neurotic, and I probably should see a therapist at some point," he starts. "But it's just that...my parents 'just moved in together' and it didn't mean anything. They never got married. It was like it was something they maybe planned to do and then just never did, and so everything just felt temporary. There was no loyalty and no reason to try and hold out or work on things. It was like they were just both waiting to find someone better, or to split because they couldn't stand it anymore."

I go to protest, *we are so not his parents*, but he won't let me.

"I know we're not like them," he assures me. "And that lots of people who live together totally get married and stay together forever and I absolutely don't judge them for it, because it really does seem like the rational thing to do. But, when I was a kid, I promised myself I would never live with anybody else until I was married. Which is lame, I know. But. I want...I want to buy towels with you. I want to fight over whose mouldy Tupperware is on the counter. I want to have a wedding and a registry and a first dance, and, hell, just a big party with all our friends."

And I wonder if I don't want that too. "I don't know, Ry..." I whisper.

His hand cups my neck and his tone is deliberate as he steamrolls ahead.

"And then I want to move into a new place, a place that's just mine and yours. Where I can pack your lunches and share your bathroom and fuck you at six a.m. I don't want to come home to empty rooms anymore, and I want it to be for real. Not just some half-assed trial period. Hell, I even want to wear a ring and say pretentious shit like 'my partner' when people ask about it, and have everyone feel envious that I've found you, when they're still single and alone. I want you to be my family: legally and otherwise. I love you. I'd do anything for you. You *know* that. Please, Niles. Please, *please* say yes."

He stares at me, begging, for a long moment. The power, unexpectedly mine, makes me uncomfortable. Finally I drag my eyes away.

"Untie me." It isn't a request.

His chest deflates but he tugs the knots loose. My arms fall, aching and helpless at my sides and I rub my wrists and lick my lips and look at him: my beautiful boy.

And then I say what is quite possibly the stupidest thing I ever could and ever will say.

"Yeah. Yeah, alright."

Because everything, every fucking little thing he just said, makes perfect sense to me.

And Rylan bulldozes me into the bed, jolting pain from my ass to my entire nervous system and I scream because it hurts like a son of a bitch, but also because I know for goddamn certain that he wants me, and will want me, and will never not want me, and, fuck it, that's all I ever wanted anyway.

- THE END -

Lightning Source UK Ltd.
Milton Keynes UK
UKOW02f2253011014

239522UK00004B/188/P